DREAMS OF FAIR WOMEN

When I was twenty-three I saw Jean Genet's notorious play, *The Balcony,* the story of a brothel where men act out their fantasies of power and cruelty among submissive whores and mirrors. As I left the theatre I was seized by a perverse obsession which has now released me from that day to this: to find, somewhere in the world, the obverse of Genet's dream, a whorehouse where women force their fantasies on the visiting men. . .

Born in London in the 1950s of mid-European parents, *Celeste Arden* has travelled widely and lived on three continents. Although she studied English Literature at Cambridge she bases her writing on her own adult experiences. She has held a variety of jobs, from waitressing in nightclubs to freelance journalism. She currently lives with a friend in Rome and is researching the Latin way of love for a new book.

D0876762

DREAMS OF FAIR WOMEN

Celeste Arden

A STAR BOOK
published by
the Paperback Division of
W.H. Allen & Co Plc

A Star Book

Published in 1987
by the Paperback Division of
W.H. Allen & Co Plc
44 Hill Street
London W1X 8LB

Printed and bound in Great Britain by
Anchor Brendon Ltd, Tiptree, Essex.

ISBN 0 352 32063 X

To G. T., *in memory*

DREAMS OF
FAIR WOMEN

When I was twenty-three I saw Jean Genet's notorious play, *The Balcony*, the story of a brothel where men act out their fantasies of power and cruelty among submissive whores and mirrors. This was in California, on a sweltering hot night. The men in the audience took off their jackets, ran with sweat and looked at their female companions with predatory eyes. I found myself recoiling from the prospect of the savage, imitative fantasies which would be acted out that night in the decorous suburbs of Santa Barbara. And as I left the theatre I was seized by a perverse obsession which has not released me from that day to this: to find, somewhere in the world, the obverse of Genet's dream, a whorehouse where women force their fantasies on the visiting men, creating the wildest rigmaroles and scenarios in their craving for satisfaction. Would men pay to enter such a place? I know *I* would.

Since then I have been searching like a miser for his

fortune. Having the means and the time to spend, I have passed years of my life in pursuit of this chimera – if such it is. Bawdy houses of Babylon, stews of Greece, houses of ill-fame, of vice, of pleasure – I could write the *Who's Whore* of brothels. At university I had studied psychology for three years, during which I followed a special course on female sexuality. Although I found plausible Freud's derogatory account of woman's sexual impulses as secondary and derivative, I remained unconvinced, always feeling that he tailored the facts to fit his prejudices. Surely the female brain – which everyone agrees to have a balance between the two hemispheres dissimilar from that of men – must respond to altogether different sexual stimuli and so, on the imaginative level, must give rise to quite different fantasies? The complicity of most women in the macho fantasies of their lovers cannot be taken as evidence against this hypothesis because this acquiescence is conditioned by a sexual culture which is predominantly male-orientated. Reasoning on these lines, I saw my self-set task as a momentous piece of research, rather than an odyssey of self-indulgence. My approach to my pleasures would be scholarly, and my experiences would enable me to write the first definitive treatise on woman's sexual imagination, based on empirical evidence!

Consequently, no country was omitted from my sexual itinerary. In Calcutta I found girl-children, lined up against the wall in a filthy hovel in ceremonial Bengali skirts – their future trousseaux? Brown breasts so small and round that I longed to cup them with wine glasses, or fit thimbles to their nipples. In Isfahan I came upon the celebrated *bordel* where the tarts have iron teeth – my arse still bears the record of that encounter. In Egypt, I paid through the nose to be allowed into an ancient palace where the whores had undergone pharaonic circumcision in their infancy. Not even the little finger could pass through their tiny, infibulated holes, nor could they feel pleasure, but their hands and tongue were more cuntlike than cunts. There, too, I picked up an exotic virus which left me in a priapic state for months on end, sick with insatiable sexual hunger. In a nameless Iron Curtain country I was serviced by the Commissar of Police's comrade-secretary on his swivelling interrogation chair – she poured vodka down my throat and stroked my prick with the barrel of his Mauser. Even in London I found novelties: in a suburb renowned for its respectability, in a bourgeois three-bedroomed house of the 1930s, I jostled on the staircase with tycoons, lords and judges for ten frantic minutes with neighbouring housewives who had told their husbands they were 'just off to the shops'. The list is endless, but . . ..

But none of these were what I sought. Even in the most fantastic situations, the prostitute was acting out what she imagined her client's fantasy to be. What about women's fantasies, whore's fantasies? (I think they are the same thing!) I wanted to be immersed, to drown in them. Wherever I travelled, I made inquiries – not an easy thing, because our language has no word to describe what I was looking for, a whorehouse where a man strives to realise the tart's most bizarre dreams, to fuck her imagination as much as her body, and to explode while submerged in her desires. You may say: Yes we sophisticates have all read Sacher-Masoch's *Venus in Furs* – what's new? That's not what I mean – I'm no masochist. But the only fantasies we have heard about for centuries have been male fantasies of the cock-

11

plugs-cunt variety. Not only are they ultimately repetitive and boring, but they ignore a whole realm of delight – which inhabits the dirtiest crevices of a woman's mind. Why shouldn't men pry into them, enjoy them and be enjoyed? But most men are hooked on the miracle of their own cocks and obsessed with where to put them, and women have been taken over by the same obsession, so that I had trouble getting directions to a female fantasy brothel. This is what I finally called it, trying to make myself understood across five continents. The result – endless misunderstandings, countless wild-goose chases. I can't pretend that I didn't enjoy them, but all the time I felt a hyper-tension which began in my stomach and spread through the nervous system. It would only be released when I found what I wanted.

One day my journey took me through Paris. I strolled along the Boulevard Pigalle on a sultry, thundery after-noon, refusing to buy postcards of negresses with donkeys. A small, gross Arab, unmistakably dressed as a pimp, asked for a light, then invited me into a doorway. On the first floor, he promised, 'are women who surpass your farthest fantasies, whose voluptuous arses and milk-white breasts . . .' I pushed past him and ran upstairs, and rang the bell outside a dirty, peeling door. After much undoing of chains and bolts – perhaps it was too early for trade – it half-opened. A frowsy red-head in a front-buttoned evening dress nodded wordlessly to me to come inside, and locked the door again.

'What kind of girl do you want?'

'I want a girl – with *imagination*. A girl who will make me do what *she* wants.'

Experience had taught me to omit the word 'fantasy',

12

which usually produced tarts with stage manners, dressed in feathers or rubber, who strutted and preened to my total embarrassment.

'I've got just the one for you. Sit down, please.'

Already anticipating failure, I sank into the broken-down chair that she offered me, with its shiny patches where green velvet had once been, and looked round at the murky hanging in the ante-room which depicted, as far as I could tell, two satyrs holding down a young girl about to be raped by an incontinently drunk Bacchus. Surely he would fall off if . . . I thought. Madame reappeared abruptly and indicated that I should follow her along the dingy corridor. With a theatrical gesture, she threw open a door. Horror of horrors! Framed in the doorway was an Amazonian woman in white leather thigh boots, black leather laced tunic, posed with one foot on the seat of a dentist's chair, and brandishing a thick riding crop. I hardly looked at her face, which had been carefully composed to imitate the snarl of a tiger.

'No. Not for me,' I said, shutting the door hastily and turning away.

'Why not?' demanded my hostess. She was extremely put out by this rejection of her tableau vivant.

'I didn't ask for *bondage*.'

'What's wrong with it? Why not try it? People pay a lot for that girl.'

She led me back to the waiting room, and pointed to the chair, determined to uncover the reason for my strange refusal before she let me go.

'I'm sure that she's got a good whip-hand. But it isn't what I asked for. That girl is enacting a *male* fantasy. She wouldn't make me do what *she* wants. She'd make me do what she thinks *I* want her to make me do. It's so

13

predictable and crass. I want a girl who has her own fantasies – don't you understand that?'

By then I was dispirited with my search, the heat and the sordidness of the appartment, and was desperate to go. Madame, astonishingly, took pity on me.

'It's an unusual requirement, but I think I understand. You're a good-looking fellow, still young, a fine strong body – yet you don't want to dominate women or force your wishes on them? Very curious. But, as it happens, I may be able to help you, because I have a contact . . . There would be *commission*, of course.'

She delicately looked away and undid the top button of her dress.

'I'll pay whatever you want. I'm not poor.'

'I can see that from your suit. But I don't take my commission in cash.'

She undid another button. Something fell into place in my head.

'I'll give you your commission however you wish. Do you want it now?'

'Can you pay now?'

She took me back down the same corridor, which seemed even dingier and mustier than before, and into a bedroom devoid of character but almost clean by comparison with the rest. I was uncertain whether I was supposed to be business-like, or to act the gigolo. Since the woman was well past fifty, plump, wrinkled and painted, but with a randy air, I decided on the more romantic role, and moved to undo the third button and slip my hand between her breasts. But she shook herself free impatiently, pulled up her dress to her waist, lay down on the bed with wide open beaver, and shut her eyes. This method of doing business aroused me at once.

I never saw her body or felt her tits – I just opened my flies, got over her, forced my cock into a surprisingly young, wet cunt, and pumped and pumped (I believe in fair payment) until the blood ran to my head. Her legs spread wider and wider – I thought she'd split, and maliciously went at it harder. Suddenly she came, shuddering and groaning, then pushed me off her so violently that I half fell off the bed. I was piqued – her animality had made me want to come.

'No,' she said, reading my thoughts. '*You* are paying *me*.'

She pulled down her dress, sat up, replaced a hairpin. As she pushed me towards the door in a sudden hurry, she whispered directions to me.

'Take the train from Montparnasse . . . at the station ask for the taxi-driver called Georges . . . tell nobody where you are going . . . the minimum stay is for a week . . . I'll ring and tell them to expect you this evening . . . *bonne chance!*'

The door closed behind me. As I went down the winding staircase, I passed an elderly man, briefcase in hand and a smile of sweet anticipation on his face. I'm sure that I knew that face from the newspapers.

The train I caught was slow, calling at every village to deposit Parisians off to their weekend homes, so I had plenty of time to anticipate what might lie in store for me. The familiar sinking feeling returned. It was too much to hope that this chance meeting with that seedy redhead would lead to the fulfilment of my randiest dreams. I envisaged a week of wearisome imprisonment and wondered if I could escape, my money intact after a quick inspection, and still get the last train back to Paris. I

15

skimmed through *Le Monde* in a desultory way. As usual, my eye was caught by the news relating to my own sexual obsession. The development of a new strain of gonorrhoea immune to all known drugs, the rape of a runaway teenager by four gendarmes in the Dordogne. The penal code of sexuality is very severe! Yet I hoped that in my search I would find a form of pleasure not followed by the ravages of disease or the temptations of violence . . . . The train stopped once again, and I had arrived.

My case was not heavy, for I had packed only a light summer suit, and was wearing another. But there was no question of walking to my destination, since all I knew was that it was a large house a few kilometres from the village. Very few passengers got out, so luckily there would be no competition for taxis. In fact, there was only one taxi waiting. The driver, gross, greasy and smoking a fat cigar, answered to the name of Georges and said, without my saying a word, 'You want the big house? Please get in.' We set off through a village of unlovely new bungalows built on sloping ramparts of earth; from their closed shutters I concluded that this was a holiday village whose season had not yet begun, although I could see no reason to linger longer than necessary in such flat, featureless countryside. Unless there were other explanations. . . . My curiosity was aroused and I plied Georges with apparently impersonal questions about the place. Most of the houses belonged to the ladies working for the big house, he told me. They went home when they were off duty. I asked whether we were going to a nearby chateau. No, he replied, not exactly. But it was the largest house in the locality and had been there long before the village. Warming to the role of cicerone, he said that it had formerly belonged to an eccentric aristocrat who, in the 1920s, was involved in a plot to restore the Kings of Spain and France and the Tsar of Russia to their respective thrones in a dramatic trans-European royalist coup. The numerous bedrooms had been constantly ready to receive the monarchs and their retinues as the last staging post on their return to power. The kitchens were always stocked with food to delight the most exigent gourmet. A fleet of Mercedes with chauffeurs had waited in endless readiness in the stables to drive the triumphant monarchs to their three destinations. The nobleman and his fellow conspirators persisted in their delusions right up till the outbreak of the second world war. After the invasion of France, German officers were billeted there ('you may notice their influence,' he said enigmatically). When the war was over, the disappointed owner abandoned his hopes and his house and retired to Monaco where he could spend his last years under a Prince if not a King. And when he died a few years back, the house was sold –

'Who bought it?' I interrupted, bored with Georges's saga.

'Madame de Rochevillier.'

'What's she like?'

'Very rich.' He said this with an air of finality as if, ashamed of his recent garrulousness, he would compensate by virtuously refusing to gossip. I found this intensely frustrating, but before the silence grew too long we entered a wooded lane and drew up before two heavy iron gates set in a tall stone arch with a strange crest on top. It seemed to consist of a crowned boar mounting a dog. The sad aristocrat's, I supposed. Georges accepted a heavy tip gracefully and drove off, having advised me to ring the doorbell several times to make sure 'she' heard. While I waited I wondered whether or not he knew the nature of Madame de Rochevillier's business. His attitude had been respectful, with none of the innuendos habitually made by taxi drivers taking you to a red light district. But then, why ask exclusively for Georges at the station? The scenario intrigued me more than I could have expected. The journey had sharpened my anticipation and I felt a sudden surge of hope. Light footsteps came down the path on the other side of the gate.

As the small door in the blank gate opened, a woman's voice asked if this was Monsieur Smith. I almost replied that it was not, having already forgotten the absurdly predictable pseudonym that I had given to the redhead.

'Yes. I hope that I am expected?'

'Madame is preparing for you even now. Please come in.'

I stepped through the door and saw a young woman dressed in the black skirt and white apron of an old-fashioned maid. She looked every inch the part – black stockings, lace shoes and long blond hair looped up and pinned back under a white mob cap. A pert, sluttish face belied her submissive politeness. She led me up a short drive through dark trees into a bright clearing with a large square lawn in the centre. At one end of the lawn stood a square, imposing house in yellow stone, three storeys high. Most of the upstairs rooms were shuttered but the ground floor windows and the large central door stood open. At the opposite side of the lawn were willow trees, masking a long, low grey stone building, while on the third side there were stables, outhouses and an elegant barn. In my mind's eye, I could see the fleet of black Mercedes filling the gravel drive which encircled the lawn. On this warm sunlit evening, the scene was timeless and tranquil, and I suddenly felt like a guest at a country houseparty rather than a man visiting a brothel.

The 'maid' said that she would take my suitcase to my room and instructed me to go into the main house, where I would find Madame. She smiled enticingly, refused a tip, and went off towards the low, grey building. With trepidation I crossed the lawn and went up the steps into the main hall. A white-haired woman was writing at a desk in the corner of the room and, hearing me, she got up and came over to greet me. When she stood, I could see that she was tall and shapely, with an almost regal bearing. Her dress was black, reminding me of the weeds worn not so long ago by Frenchwomen of her age, but tailored in rich brocade – haute couture, no mistake. When I saw her face to face I was struck by her beauty. She must have been seventy, yet the wrinkles were scarcely visible: one saw only a fine, haughty face with high carved cheekbones and huge blue eyes. Shaking my hand, she spoke to me in English.

'Welcome, Monsieur Smith. We are always pleased to entertain an English gentleman here, even one going under the name of Smith. I hope that you will find your stay satisfying. Dinner will be in half-an-hour, and I hope that you will do me the honour of joining me, so that I can explain things to you. Perhaps you would like to go to your room and have a shower before dinner? Your room is Number 3, Virginie will show you.'

The maid was already behind me again, as I sensed from the stale, musky smell which surrounded her. I followed her round the lawn to the grey building, noticing now how short and how tight her skirt was, and how it rippled over each buttock as she swayed along.

19

We went into a hall, and she showed me into a room on the right, which turned out to be a suite of rooms – bathroom, sittingroom and bedroom, decorated in the muted good taste of the best hotels of the 1930s. Perhaps this had been destined for the Tsar? At first the rooms seemed devoid of any unusual feature, but on looking round more carefully, I noticed a strange device embedded in the wall of the bedroom at hip-level. It looked like a cross between a cassette player and a camera lens. What was it? I asked Virginie.

'You do not know, Monsieur? It is a television closed-circuit transmitter.'

'But what is it for?'

'The girls may want to watch you from time to time. It transmits the picture direct to their rooms.'

'How do I switch it off?'

'You cannot. It operates all the time.'

She curtseyed ironically and exited, leaving behind a trail of sour musk and a resolution forming in my mind that, whatever my main purpose here, I would enact a few below-stairs fantasies with her when she came to make my bed. Then I decided to take a shower, but the presence of another silent camera in the bathroom added a new dimension to the experience. Imagining that all over the big house girls would be scrutinising me and discussing my shape and size, I lingered over undressing, and stretched my limbs with a new sensation of self-importance. Fearing to disappoint them, I frigged myself hard in the passage between the rooms which I hoped was invisible to the all-seeing eye, and went into the bathroom bolt upright. For a long time I stood in front of the full-length mirror beside the bath, playing with myself lazily, pulling and shaking my cock, which responded by growing even bigger, and turning deepest purple. Had I passed the test? By the time I started to run the shower I was in a state of itching excitement, fancying that the device was a two-way transmitter and that I could hear whispers of astonishment and admiration coming from many bedrooms. I stepped into the shower, and when I looked for the soap I found a huge block of peach-coloured soap shaped like an arse, with an enticing cavity in it. Laughing at such consideration on my hostess's part, I tried it – it fitted my swollen prick like a soft, insinuating glove. On and off, on and off, I moved it with a slow sensuousness calculated to please the invisible spectators, and ended by pleasing myself. My cock strained and rebelled under the slimy pressure until I thought it would burst the soap asunder, and finally I spurted all I had into the warm slippery hole. For a long time I basked in the shower, stroking and rinsing every inch of my body, which glowed with the release of tension. Slowly and narcissistically, I dried myself with the velvety bath sheet, and appraised myself. The mirror showed me a tall athletic body: muscular limbs, elegant hands and feet, and a slight tan. My cock is of the kind which is naturally large, even in repose, and so I fail according to Leonardo's ideal proportions, a failure which brings some rewards, however. The curious feeling of being on approval made me more appreciative of myself than before. With satisfaction, I dressed for dinner.

'I hope you have not tired yourself out,' Madame de Rochevillier greeted me, as I was shown into the dining room by Virginie, adding innocently, 'the journey from Paris is very tedious.'

With some formality, we sat facing each other across a

circular glass table, in white basket chairs with high, peacock-feather backs. The room was light and spacious and seemed to have been furnished in the Spanish style, with a tiled floor, opulent rugs, white furniture and a tame jungle of plants under the windows. We were dining alone, somewhat to my surprise, since I had hoped that my future harem would put in an appearance. But only Virginie was present, in her equivocal servant role. She had substituted a lace apron and stiletto heels for her day wear, which raised her tempting rump, and exaggerated its rhythmic movement as she brought in each course when Madame de Rochevillier rang a small handbell. I fancied that she pressed herself unnecessarily against my left shoulder as she served me with sauce for the asparagus, and looked at me from under her long lashes with eyes that were glittering black stones. No hired whore in a filthy hotel room had ever conveyed to me an impression of such sleaziness as did the inaptly named Virginie in her prim maid's costume.

'My first husband was an English lord, you know. As you will see, we observe many English customs here. I often take four o'clock tea,' drawled Madame de Rochevillier in her engaging French accent. 'I find the English style very special.'

I agreed for the sake of politeness, although I have always found the style, the cuisine and the lovemaking of my compatriots monotonous. True to her word, an English roast was served for the main dish, although the cheese and profiteroles which followed were unmistakably French, and restored my good humour. Madame clearly enjoyed a good Bordeaux, and offered me the decanter so often that I soon felt myself getting light-headed. It was a strange experience to eat with this elderly woman who acted the grande dame and urbane hostess and exchanged small talk while my mind constantly wandered towards the obscene produce which she was to sell me. But her conversation was agreeable and her way of speaking was what I associated with far younger women – direct, frank and even unbridled. She asked how I had heard of her house, and said that one day I must recount my adventures en route. I tried to find out more details of her life but her replies were evasive: she talked of travel, of cocktail parties, and dropped the names, most unknown to me, of members of her elevated circle in French society. I wondered again whether I had not arrived accidentally at an *haut bourgeois* country house where they were too polite to turn away an imposter, and entertained him like an honoured guest.

Over coffee and brandy my fears were dispelled when my hostess's manner suddenly became brisk and businesslike.

'My second husband was a French nobleman. When he died a few years back, I bought this house as a pastime. I call it '*ma folie*' – my folly, you would say, but for us it has the stronger sense of obsession or madness. My colleague, Madame Mirabelle, sent you here because your desires seemed to match our requirements. This is not a public brothel and very few people know of its existence. Like this, we avoid unsuitable clients. That is why, when you leave, I shall ask you to give your word of honour to maintain this secrecy.'

I assured her at once that I would be silent.

'Good. And now you will want to know the terms and conditions of your stay here and what you can expect in return. You are to remain for a week, and the cost will be thirty thousand francs to be paid in advance – tomorrow morning, unless you change your mind tonight. In the house there are ten bedrooms – in each, a different girl, with different requirements. I suggest that you visit one or two a day – if you did more, you would exhaust yourself, and it is my duty to the girls to make sure that you are on good form. The one rule of the house is that when you enter a girl's room you should submit to her wishes, however extreme, and for as long as she wants. Any attempt to impose your desires on her, or to act in ways which she forbids, will result in your immediate departure, or in a suitable penalty. To keep up your strength, you will need frequent, heavy meals.' Here, I had visions of the brides-to-be in primitive tribes being fattened on buttermilk and too obese to move, waiting in bed, to submit to their husbands' will.

'Virginie will look after you at breakfast, you will lunch alone unless one of the girls invites you to eat with her, and you will dine with me. At present you are our only guest, but I am expecting another in a few days' time, and you will meet him one way or another, no doubt. Have you any questions?'

My mind was focussed on the prospect of those ten delights, and I said that I had nothing to ask.

'Well, perhaps you would like to visit the first room now? Goodbye until tomorrow and *bon appetit*!'

Reverting to the formal hostess, Madame shook hands with me and stalked out of the room, sending in Virginie who asked me to follow her. We walked down a long passage to the right and climbed what must once have been the servants' staircase. The ground floor of the house had been somewhat austere, with tile or stone floors and sparsely furnished, but the first floor was another world. A thick gold carpet stretched the length of the corridor, which seemed to run through the centre of the house with rooms leading off on both sides. The walls were covered with Chinese paper, with exotic fauna and caged parrots staring down at me. We went a few paces, then Virginie stopped and pointed to a green baize door.

'You are expected. Just go in.'

Her swaying arse retreated down the corridor, diverting me temporarily from the task ahead.

The First Room

I opened the double doors and went in, my head throbbing with anticipation. At first I thought that there had been a mistake because just inside the door rose a tall wall, sealing off the rest of the room and leaving me in a narrow passage. The false wall ended a few feet below the ceiling, and light seeped over from the window. Baffled, I moved towards the wall and, touching it, discovered it to be canvas tightly stretched across wooden struts, painted to represent an old stone wall. Theatre scenery in fact. A lost memory stirred in my mind, but I could not think what I was reminded of. Then a peal of inviting laughter came from the other side, followed by silence, then the self-indulgent sigh of a woman caressing herself. I was intrigued, if annoyed by this game of hide-and-seek.

Until then I had only regarded the wall at eye level. Now I looked down slightly, and saw a series of holes of irregular size at various heights. A flash of colour moved

27

behind one of them, and I knelt down to peer through: looking back at me was a pale pink, diamond-shaped cunt, surrounded by a fringe of curling dark hair. She must be bending down. It seemed to smile at me. Although I had just eaten, my appetite returned. I salivated. I put out my tongue and reached through the canvas to touch those perfect, sculptured lips. A taste of salt and then of honey. My saliva ran. I pursed my lips and forced my mouth through the canvas aperture to suck thirstily at that tauntingly mouthlike creature, and twist the sticky hairs round my teeth and tongue. The cunt moved provocatively, sometimes so far away that my outstretched tongue could scarcely reach it, sometimes pressing itself against the wall, seeming suddenly available and vulnerable. But the lips remained closed together, purselike. While tonguing this disembodied sex, I had almost forgotten the demands of my own body, but now my cock pressed uncomfortably against my flies, demanding its freedom, so I released it and squeezed it hard, then went back to sucking and licking through the hole, while I rubbed myself against the wall. I wanted the fountain of pleasure to run – my tongue tried to part the tightly shut lips to drink – but suddenly the source moved away from the hole and vanished from sight. More laughter.

I looked through the hole again in time to see a flash of bare leg moving out of my restricted field of vision to the right. I stood up again and moved in the corresponding direction, and suddenly noticed the omnipresent camera's eye on the wall at the end of my confined space. So I was to be a spectacle all the time? For the benefit of my audience, I thrust my stiff tool, now straining to be vertical, through another crevice which appeared at just the right height. This was the strangest sensation yet: I could no longer see my cock, it had an unruly life of its own on the other side of the wall where I could not be, yet despite its separation from me I felt its every twinge and throb ten times more strongly than when I could see and handle it. After a minute or so, a hand laden with something cool and creamy took my cock, caressed and coated it, peeling back the foreskin, tickling and greasing the knob. Powerless to affect what happened, a prisoner of the wall, I writhed ecstatically at the end of my cock.

The proportions of my body, the correct order and priority of my limbs and organs were all disturbed, dislocated. I closed my eyes and swam. When I opened them again, I noticed some higher holes in the wall which were some way above that through which my cock had travelled. The canvas rippled slightly and suddenly, sure enough, a tantalising nipple, all alone, appeared through a tiny round hole – swollen, erect, flushed dark. So I took it and rolled it between my fingers, first gently, like rolling a cigarette, and then pinched it for all I was worth. A gasp from the other side, and the hand slid over my cock faster. The wall shook again – and suddenly a whole round breast forced itself through a hole beside the first nipple and hung there, constricted by the space into a white, spherical fullness that made me yearn and twitch on the other side of the wall, while on this side I feasted my eyes. The breast seemed to glow in the deepening twilight. Contorting myself so as to maintain contact through all the three holes, I began to lick it, starting at the edge and moving in every-decreasing circles towards the nipple, as hard and protuberant as its twin. It stood out a full inch from the pale, soft flesh, begging to be bitten, subdued – so I bit it with the sharpest teeth, again and again. Screams of delight from my invisible mistress.

So for a long time, we stood and moved in unison, unseen by each other yet inextricably attached at three points of double bliss. We must have resembled a sex encyclopaedia with illustrations where arrows point to the erogenous zones. But as my body floated from plateau to plateau of pleasure, my mind became obstinately active. Who could it be on the other side? Could her whole body match up to the perfection of the tiny portions which had offered themselves to me? Would I see her face? I imagined that it might be the suggestive Virginie, divested of her skin-tight skirt but modestly wearing her lace apron and stilettos. But this body was surely younger, fresher, tighter than the ragged, oft-used body of Virginie (as I envisaged her), nor could I smell her dust and old perfume. This was a new girl. Perhaps she was young and ingenuous, and it was modesty which made her present herself behind the wall. I pressed myself closer to the canvas, seized with a strong desire to see and know this tantalising whore. The whole structure was flimsy, the canvas thin. I could push a fist through it, tear down the wall and at last touch all over the body whose discrete parts had roused me to such a pitch of frenzy, mind and body. To execute this plan, I took my right hand from her nipple and pressed it hard against the canvas, which bulged outwards.

'*Non, non, NON!*' came from the other side, and nipple, breast and hand disappeared instantly. There was silence, and I remembered Madame's threat that my pleasures would be cut short if I tried to impose my own desires. I also recalled my ultimate obsession, to live a

30

woman's fantasy. My attempt to see the girl was the destruction of her fantasy, and my pleasure: perhaps she would show herself to me later, or never. I must wait. So I called back in French that I promised not to tear down the wall and that if she would only come back I would do anything she asked.

I heard movements, then again that bell-like laughter, this time coming from near a large hole low down on the left. Again I knelt to look, and saw an enchanting sight – two plump, globular buttocks divided by a deep fissure! This time the aperture was large, so that I was able to thrust through both my hands, and got to work on those cheeky contours, now stroking them with a feathery touch, now palpating them roughly, finally wrenching them apart to discover the dark hole, puckered like a rosebud, into which I forced my largest finger, corkscrewing it around like a male pig in rut, while the bum which it impaled moved in a wild, elliptical dance. A sudden spasm shook the pale globes, they tore away from me, and I heard a hoarse cry, and another, and another. Then nothing.

By now it must have been ten o'clock and night had fallen, although the room was dimly lit beyond the wall and the many holes threw vague, irregular patches of yellow light on the outer wall, my side of the room. I was still in a state of hard, unrelieved lust, titillated beyond my randiest dreams, and simultaneously drained and exhausted by the effort to satisfy the enigmatic demands of the bawd's strange fantasy. As I wondered what could happen next, and which hole would become the channel for the discharge of my bounding energy, the lights in the room beyond suddenly went out and I was left, nonplussed, in warm darkness. After a few moments, a hazy blue light appeared on the wall of the room facing me, which gradually focussed and took form. A picture appeared. From the wood and canvas structure in the background, I realised that I was seeing the secret of the room beyond the wall. In front of it paraded a young girl shaped like an hour-glass. The parts of her that I had been allowed to see and touch were moulded together in a fluid, perfect shape, joined by a tiny waist. Her full, small breasts were taut and high. Her compact bum was carried high on shapely thighs and her legs were slender. Long, dark hair hung over her shoulders, obscuring her face as she bent forward and matched her cunt to the first hole in the mock-wall. She crouched there, swaying slightly, holding her breasts in both hands. Then, as she straightened up and walked away, I saw my cock protrude through the wall, jerking erect. She moved out of the picture, then came back with a large pot of cream which she spread copiously on the intruder, spattering some on the floor as she went to work. Now she turned her back and used her other hand to force her nipple out to me, then her breast, and stood for a long time, her right hand rapidly moving to and fro as she rubbed me. Afterwards she moved away quickly and turned round. Now I could see her face which seemed like a collage of the dismembered parts of her body which were so familiar: plump-cheeked like her arse, with a diamond-shaped mouth, parted (as she shouted 'No!') to show small, sharp teeth. A long, straight nose, then round eyes circled with kohl, whore's eyes in an adolescent face which had not yet lost its puppy-fat. Then she squatted down again, hair falling in cascade in front, and I saw her bury her fingers in the dark maiden-hair, as my hands came through the wall and grasped her buttocks. How I wished that the silent camera had been fitted with a zoom lens! The mime continued, and I found I was sweating all over as I watched until at last she fell forward, spreadeagled on the floor, and the picture faded leaving me in total darkness again.

The silence from the other side had been so long and heavy that I thought that maybe she had no more use for me and that I should leave. But as I felt for the door a bright spotlight was switched on. A pencil-thin stream of light, emanating from high on the wall above the door, picked out one of the holes at thigh level, and illuminated once more that tempting cunt. Now the lips were reddened and open, and I could even see her liquid, glistening on the edge of the dark passage. But now I had no time or energy to spare for savouring that sweetness with my tongue, or for teasing love-play. I moved close to the wall and stuck two peremptory fingers into that tiny entrance, which widened avidly as if to engulf my hand. I thought I heard a sigh of pleasure so I meanly pulled them out again. This time I had made up my mind to be brutally male, and to come as and when I wanted. My prick was like an over-ripe plum, ready to burst, and I felt that only a few seconds separated me from the explosion. I wanted to punish her hiddenness by climaxing after a few savage strokes, leaving her hanging over the precipice and unable to fall.

But when I got inside her, the strange spell cast by her fantasy washed over me again and paralysed my will. Again I was split into two. My cock, a long, long way away, wallowing in a deep, hot pool, had achieved the unity which it sought and, oblivious to me, went on leaping and dancing crazily in its private world. I myself, on this side of the wall, ached for the physical contact only permitted to my member, and this ache paradoxically sharpened the pleasure of my rival down there. Perhaps she felt the same jealousy of her cunt – who knows? The limiting of erotic experience to one part of the body by the concealment of the rest increases the appetite, so say the psychologists. We see this truth in its absurdest form when, in a Victorian novel, the heroine raises her skirt to reveal her ankle and her suitor falls into a swoon of delight. In my case now, physical separation and total concealment were an unbelievably powerful combination which concentrated my desire into something thin, sharp and laser-like. The only focus of the sexual impulses diffused throughout the body was my cock in her cunt, and through one into the other poured an electric charge. My hands fumbled over the dark wall, trying to feel her through the coarse material, and I was half sobbing with the effort of fucking in that ridiculous position – on my knees, through a hole in a pantomime wall. I saw nothing now, but I felt a warm flood rush down her milky way as she became fully aroused, and she started to cry out. Before I drowned in that delectable juice, I sent my spunk gushing into her, with a great shout.

For a long time I sat on the floor, my head reeling. Maybe I dozed, because when I opened my eyes the lights had gone out again. I groped for the door and let myself out into the corridor which was also in darkness except for a small, dim bulb at the far end. I went back the way I had come and left through the main door, which apparently was not locked at night, crossing the lawn in the light of a sliver of moon and finally regaining my room with a sense of profound tiredness. Only then did I look at my watch and see that it was two in the

34

morning. Had our love game really lasted five hours? I took out my notebook and tentatively wrote down my first observation on the nature of women's fantasy: 'Far more unified and prolonged than the fantasy of men, demanding a more complete absorption of the other in the act, but also affording a deeper, longer satisfaction'. By way of an epilogue, I stuck my tongue out at the late-night viewers and, falling into bed, went fast asleep.

On waking, I sometimes have the impression that a malicious demon has wiped the slate of my mind clean during the night. It felt like this the following morning when I woke with a blank mind, unable at first to locate myself in time and space. Where was I? Had the crazy experience of the previous night been a long wet dream? I was surprised to hear a tap at the door and to see Virginie, looking cleaner and more matinal (I thought), enter with a breakfast tray. She asked insinuatingly if the bed was comfortable. While she arranged the tray on a table beside the bed, she stared shamelessly at my bare shoulders, then reached out a hand as if to help me sit up and lightly brushed it over the hair on my chest.

'Mademoiselle Florence asks if you will take lunch with her in the Green Room,' she said.

So the whores chose to see me when they felt like it! Nothing could have pleased me better. I asked her to thank Mademoiselle Florence and to say that I would be delighted to lunch with her.

'I shall leave you then.' She lingered in the doorway. Whether this was an invitation to contradict her I did not know, but I still felt too exhausted from my researches of the night before to make the effort, so I reached for my cup, and she turned and left. After strong coffee and croissants, I felt much better and had a shower, almost forgetting the camera this time. I decided to stroll into the village, since it seemed that no demands were to be made on me that morning. I found the door in the iron gate unlocked and open, though nobody was about, and retraced the road along which Georges had driven me, for a mile or so before I came to the first outlying houses of the village. Again, the unearthly calm of a ghost town, with not a soul in the streets. A few houses were unshuttered this morning, and one even had a washing line hanging out, but the silent inactivity began to oppress me. I walked round the whole village, which did not take long, exploring all the interconnecting streets. Some houses seemed better established than others, with small flowering trees in the front gardens, while other virgin gardens were still mounds of brown earth awaiting the bulldozer. As well as greenery, the village lacked shops, a church and even a bar – remarkable! It could only be described as desolate, despite the money that had obviously been lavished on these holiday houses. Just as I thought of turning back, an elderly man appeared from the back of a newly-built house, dressed in workman's dungarees and carrying a spade. I greeted him, determined to extract a little human contact and possibly some information about the deserted village. He dropped his spade and came over to the garden gate, probably as pleased as I was to see another human being and to have the chance of a chat. I asked him whether there was a bar in the village, although I knew the answer already. No such luck, he replied, the nearest cognac was a good five kilometres away. I expressed amazement at the absence of such facilities from what was evidently an affluent village.

'Ah, well, that's because nobody lives here.'

'But what about the people who own the houses?'

'Most of the ladies stay up in the big house when they come down from Paris. Just sometimes one of them brings a friend for the weekend, and then she stays in her own bungalow. If you ask me, it's a damn good tax dodge.'

He was keen to gossip, but I soon realised that he had no information, and no idea, about what went on in the big house. He came from the nearby town where the railway station was, and only came over to do odd jobs for the ladies, who paid him well, he said. We chatted a little longer about the tedium of village life, the cost of living and the weather, and then parted. I walked back trying to make some sense of the few details that I had learnt. The obvious conclusion was that the prostitutes at the big house were not full-time residents, but divided their time between there and the more conventional brothels. Probably it was a pleasant pastime to come and unleash their fantasies here for a large fee, after submitting willy-nilly to the whims of their clients in Paris. But why should they bother to own houses which they so rarely used? Tax concessions were an unlikely reason – nor would I have thought that such women were investing in these properties in order to retire later in life to a Sunset City populated entirely by other ladies of the profession. The mystery of the village was far less enthralling than the thought of what might await me in the Green Room, but it nevertheless gnawed away at the periphery of my consciousness.

When I reached the iron gates again, I realised that it was still only eleven o'clock, and lunch, presumably, did not begin until one. Reluctant to return to the boredom

37

of my room and the scrutiny of unknown eyes, I resolved to explore as much of the ground floor as paying guests were permitted to see. I passed through the empty ante-room where Madame had received me the previous day. With its antique furniture and heavy decorative style, the room looked more like part of a museum than a private house. Leading out of it on the left was a passage at the end of which double doors stood open. As I reached them, I could see row upon row of leather-bound books and some inviting wing-chairs in dark brown velvet. This library looked so much like an English gentleman's club that I warmed to it immediately, and planned to spend all my spare time exploring its shelves, since the village would evidently not provide much entertainment, let alone the flat, dull countryside which surrounded it.

Without looking at the title, I picked out a heavy volume from the shelf nearest the door and, sitting down, opened it. It was dated 1795 and was written in German by one Luther von Liebknecht, and entitled – as far as my faltering knowledge of the language allowed me to translate it – *Some Observations on the Curious Sexual Habits of Insects and the Lower Invertebrates*. I did not attempt to read the text, but the engravings of exotic mating rituals were very intriguing, the more so because of their high degree of magnification. The male flea puncturing his mate at random in his haste, and thereby creating a new, perfectly serviceable, sexual channel, held my attention for a long time. More sinis-terly, there was an action picture of the benign money spider dismembering her mate after the act of consum-mation, her fearsome mandibles enlarged a hundred times. The curious thing is that human beings have so jealously appropriated the sexual act to themselves that they resist the idea that other forms of life do the same thing. The idea that birds engage in courtship, or pigs in love-play, is abomination to most people; they preserve their distance and superiority by coining special, derogatory words for the sex act between animals: 'coupling', 'covering', 'rutting' and so on. And, hypocritically, they continue to think of the sexual practices of animals as *perverse*! I never discovered from Herr Liebknecht what the special term is for the copulation of the lower invertebrates, and after a time I was bored with its graphic but unmoving pictures, and went to look for something more pertinent to my own state of mind. Further exploration showed that all the books in the first section of the library were about sexual topics. Some twentieth-century works such as Masters and Johnson had been bound in matching antique leather and added to the lower shelves, but I was astonished at the number of old books on the subject. Our ancestors were less prudish than I had imagined.

I sat down at a table with a French book on the nature of women's dreams. This dated from the early nineteenth century and seemed extremely naive by comparison with Freud, but I decided to read a little to pass the time. The author, Jacques Delamare – a man, of course – had an interesting hypothesis. 'Since most women are constantly kept in a state of subjection by their fathers or husbands from an early age,' he wrote, 'their dreams seek to compensate by representing power and domination'. He gave a lot of examples of women's dreams recounted to him in which they saw themselves as soldiers, kings or similar power figures. He went on to relate his theory – rather wildly, I thought – to the rise of witchcraft, where women are omnipotent and keep men in fear and subjection. For Delamare, this was clearly an inversion of the natural order, and an example of concrete dream fulfilment. But I thought of witch-ducking and hot branding irons, and marvelled at how quickly men had suppressed this Saturnalia. However, I felt obscurely – without bothering to formulate why – that if Delamare's theory had a grain of truth it must have some bearings on the goings-on in this house.

Suddenly I noticed that it was twelve-thirty, and remembered that I had to pay Madame de Rochevillier if I was to be permitted to stay – and by now all thoughts of a quick escape had vanished. I was relishing the prospect of the week ahead with a boundless appetite. The house was still silent, but I went in search of Madame, knocking at every door, and finally heard 'Entrez' in that unmistakeable, rich voice. The room was clearly her study, and she was sitting at an immense oak desk covered with files and papers. There were also two telephones and an intercom, and a small square box like a miniature television which I imagined to be the audio-visual apparatus which received the pictures transmitted by the cameras. Only the old-world setting – more books, pictures and high-backed leather chairs – and the glimpse of trees and lawn outside the window detracted from the impression that this was the office of a prosperous business-woman. Madame greeted me courteously and asked me to sit down. Today she was dressed in a cream canvas suit, simply cut, which made her seem younger and less austere than in the forbidding black dress.

'I hope you had a pleasant evening?'

'Very agreeable, thank you.' I was embarrassed by

this clinical and dutiful inquiry after the activities of the night before which, for all I knew, she had watched on the screen in front of her, avidly or disapprovingly. It was like the vicar asking circumlocuitously about your sexual habits when you go to arrange your wedding. I said that I had come to pay, and asked if she would object to a cheque.

'Since I am dealing with an Englishman, Monsieur *Smith*, that will be quite acceptable. Your word is your bond, n'est-ce pas?'

I had, of course, forgotten that my cheques had my true name printed on them, and felt myself turning red as I handed it to her, but she only smiled ironically as she looked at it. I was wondering whether I was expected to stay and exchange pleasantries, when the green telephone rang. After a brief conversation, she turned to me and said that Mademoiselle Florence was hungry now, and asked me to go up if I was ready. As if by magic, Virginie simultaneously appeared at the door to escort me to the Green Room. This punctilious organisation and the unseen mechanisms which governed my whereabouts and actions made me feel very strange – bereft of will, a passive plaything for these women. Virginie may have been piqued at my morning lethargy because she led me up to the first floor in silence. I was so looking forward to my lunch that I scarcely noticed her.

The Green Room

Mademoiselle Florence came to open the door herself and stood in the doorway surveying me carefully, face-to-face. Apparently she approved of what she saw, for she invited me in. What I saw was a long mass of black curly hair, unkempt, gipsyish, and a plump, olive-skinned face with full lips and white, sharp teeth. She must have been in her thirties and was like a magnificent Spanish señora, past the age of innocence but still in her physical prime; as I looked down at her body, I almost expected to see the full skirt of a dancer. In fact she was wearing a tight black boiler suit, patterned with silver zips, which outlined her shape like a body stocking, showing full breasts and bottom, all in ideal proportion. Although I am not specially fond of the capacious, blouzy women that Rubens immortalised, after so many experiences with sulky, sour-faced whores, it was a delight to have this generously large woman laughing and smiling at me as she led me into her sanctum. She

43

seemed so full of life and inner joy, that I could hardly believe her to be a prostitute. The room was, naturally, painted and furnished in green, which reflectcd the brightness of the foliage of the trees outside the large double window. There were easy chairs, a television, an empty bookshelf, but no bed, though I noticed an interconnecting door in one wall. But the centrepiece was a large, square pinewood table, already crowded with plates of hors d'oeuvres and covered serving dishes. Beside it, stood a trolley with two bottles of champagne in an ice bucket, and a plate overflowing with fruit. Florence took my hand and led me to one of the two larged carved pine chairs drawn up to the table, and sat me down.

She had not spoken yet, but when she did, her voice was strong and warm, almost caressing, and her accent *haut Parisien*.

'Well, Monsieur Smith, it is nice to meet you in person. I hope you have a good appetite today as well. I would like to get to know you a little over lunch, so please serve yourself and let us start.'

She opened the first bottle of champagne with masculine confidence, and gave me some in a giant, balloon-shaped glass. I took a little cold meat and some *crudités* and started to eat, but I was in a curious state of mind. The idea of talking to a whore, of 'getting to know her' before the act, had never crossed my mind, nor had I ever met one who had such a sociable attitude towards her client. Consequently, I found myself at a loss as to what to say or how to act. The women's behaviour in this house seemed to oscillate between the extremes of lewdness and formality. Which was it to be today? Florence resolved the question almost immediately.

'I enjoyed your performance last night so much! I masturbated in front of the TV until I fell asleep.'

Unanswerable – but luckily she went on, 'All of us have different fantasies, you see, but we share each other's as well. Women are like men in that way, even if men don't like to think so. When I saw that great tool of yours, poking through that hole, I really wished I was in Julie's place, and she says she had a great time behind her wall. But then, I like to *see* the men I'm going to fuck. Would you like to take off your clothes?'

So the process of getting to know me verbally was relatively short – I had not yet said a word! However, she then said, 'No, not just yet, have some more sausage, and some pâté. I like to see a man's stomach swollen with food, especially when he is too thin, like you.' Again, I visualised the buttermilk brides, and I obediently took some more and set to eating as fast as I could. Florence herself emptied her piled plate with great gusto, and seemed to me like a female Bacchus as she refilled her plate and glass bountifully. As she ate, more slowly and sensuously now, she asked me what I thought of the tarts in the Paris brothels, but scarcely had I begun to answer when she put down her knife and fork and came and stood behind me, and took off my jacket.

'Keep on talking,' she said, and I stumbled on with invented descriptions of the sexy but ill-tempered black whores of the Rue Saint-Denis, and the sleek, well-fed, over-paid call-girls of Avenue Foch, as she removed my tie and unbuttoned the top of my shirt, slipping her hands inside and stroking my chest lingeringly. She took my nipples, first one then the other, between her fingers and teased them, squeezing and twisting. Not many women remember that men's breasts are sensitive too – alas. A tingling sensation spread outwards over my whole body. My nipples, and not only my nipples, at once became full and stiff, and I tried to get up from my chair to take hold of Florence. But she said, 'Don't move,' and swiftly undid my belt. She opened my trousers as she had uncorked the champagne, with an air of knowing exactly what to do and how to get what she wanted. She made me stand up to take off my trousers, and muttered something crude in surprise as she saw my liberated cock jump up. Then I had to sit down again while she leant over my shoulder and stroked my chest, belly and thighs, occasionally passing the back of her hand across my cock. With her so close, I could smell hair and breath, sweet with champagne, and now and then a hint of rank animal sweat which stimulated my senses more than exotic perfume. Her breasts rested heavily on my shoulders, but the multiple zips on her tunic grazed my back as she moved. I was in suspense: this was the prelude to what? Would I ever get my hands on all that voluptuous flesh?

'I think we shall have the next course now,' she said. She moved all the dishes to one side of the table, and told me to lie flat on the table. Like an automaton, I did what she asked, at the same time feeling the dreadful power-lessness of the naked in front of the clothed. Postlapsarian Adam and Eve standing before God, or the wretched queues of naked Jews filing in front of their Nazi torturers – undressed, we all feel the same primal weakness and shame, and bow to the authority of the man who is clothed, and hence invulnerable. But although Florence in her black semi-uniform had just such authority over me, I sensed that she had no sadistic intentions. Her seductive, laughing mouth as she placed me in position on the table, invited me to forget my shame and join in her pleasure.

I could hear her uncovering two of the dishes on the table, and felt a sudden warm wetness on my stomach. I raised my head to look and saw that my stomach had become a plate, and Florence was ladling more and more stew on to it. Such a strange sensation could not be called primarily sexual, but when Florence pulled up her chair, took her knife and fork again and started eating delicately off my stomach, with the air of one eating off Royal Doulton with silver cutlery, I was amused and aroused at the same time. Now and again she offered me a titbit speared on the point of her knife, of what turned out to be a very tasty *boeuf bourguignon*, but mainly she fed herself and left me in an appetising state of hunger. Then she threw aside her knife and fork, bent her head over my body and started guzzling like a pig, burying her face in my stomach, smearing it all over with the food. All I could see was her wild mane of hair and tense, bent body in black.

As this Rabelaisian slut gorged herself, the stew spread out and slopped over my cock. When at last she had eaten her fill, she began to lick me clean systematically, at first excavating my navel with her tongue, then cleaning my awakening sex with long, insinuating strokes, and finally sucking every vestige of gravy from round the foreskin. This gave me such a hard-on that I sat up and reached out to pull her to me, but she moved away still licking her lips, opened the second bottle of champagne and held out another glass to me.

'Did you enjoy the main course?' she asked. I said that I had not had enough and was still hungry.

'Then we shall move on to the fruit. Do you know how to suck the mango?' I hoped that she was referring to the position of that name in the *Kamasutra* – the forty-seventh, if I remember rightly – but she produced an enormous, over-ripe, yellow mango, cut a hole in the top and proceeded to squeeze and rub its sweet-smelling, slimy contents all over my body. She massaged me with a probing touch which discovered erotic nerves that had never existed before. Smiling to herself, and taking no more notice of me than if I had been baker's dough, she squeezed and kneaded my armpits, my nipples, my balls, spreading the sweet mess everywhere. I no longer knew whether my enforced passivity was delight or torture – but I longed to seize her, to drag her onto the table among the dirty plates where she belonged, and to inflict the same casually stimulating treatment on her. But that was against the rules. I shut my eyes and enjoyed the rhythmic rubbing – and now she was licking me again all over, then sucking in her breath sharply, creating little vacuums that tugged at my over-sensitive skin, or nibbling at the loose bag of skin round my balls. Her liberal use of her teeth created a delightful sense of danger down there. Since I could not see, I did not know what might happen next, and feared that the greedy, randy bitch would make her next course off my cock.

My fear increased when, after a pause. I heard her doing something with a knife, and she took my cock in one hand. A moment of panic, and I opened my eyes and raised my head in time to see her slipping the great mango skin over it like a sheath, having removed the stone. For a long time she masturbated me with the slithering skin, a cool, blissful sensation which brought me to the brink of pleasure. While she rubbed and stroked, she kept up an obscenely abusive commentary, which often escaped my knowledge of idiomatic French 'Look how the velvet banana swells, watch it growing . . . now you are stiff like a stag . . . a bag of spunk which I'm going to burst . . . I'll puncture you with a pin and you'll collapse like a balloon . . . no, I think I'll wait, I'll swallow you up inside me and explode you in there!'

Now I was twitching all over, and crying out uncontrollably, and wanting her to stop, and to go on for ever. Abruptly, she took away her hand. In a voice warm with solicitude she said to me, as to a child, 'Ah, but look, you're all *dirty*. We must wash you.' Before I could stop her, she took the half-empty bottle and poured it out over me, giving me a cold shock. She swirled it over my body with her hands, and I could feel the bubbles bursting as it ran off me on to the table. I regretted the champagne, but not the sensation. The insatiable Florence bent down again to drink the dregs from the hollows and crevices of my body, noisily. This was evidently the end of bacchanals, and I began to feel chilly, soiled and hungry. Perhaps she sensed this, for with great charm she smiled at me and helped me up off the table, taking my hands. 'Now we shall give you a proper wash.' She took me through the adjoining door into what I had expected to be the bedroom, but was in fact a bathroom. The walls were black, as was the bath and basin. A black blind kept out the day, and a series of spotlights, reflected in mirrors projecting from every wall at strange angles, created multiple reflections and beams and tangents of light.

Florence made me stand in the bath while she washed me down with a hand shower. During this ritual, I could not refrain from touching myself up, as I had when a small boy in the nursery bathtub, and she seemed not to mind this at all. Her expression was one of constant amusement, as if her profession was very comic, and playing with me was the biggest joke of all. She helped me to dry myself maternally, with a large black towel, then shut the bathroom door, and stood facing me, her mane of hair tossed back, surrounded by ten reflections of herself, all wearing provocative smiles.

'Now that I know you better,' she said, 'You can do what you want with me here. As you see, there is no food in the bathroom, so you must use your imagination.'

I was daunted by this unexpected call to action after so long a period of passivity; the bathroom and its mirrored illusions made me feel giddy and claustrophobic. But I steadied myself against the towel-rail and considered her with what I hoped was a rapacious look. What she had said was not, however, an invitation to free inventive activity. Clearly she had something in mind that I should do. I was still taking orders!

For several minutes we stood facing each other, wrestlers about to come to grips, and I slowly looked her body up and down. Of course, *the zips!* So defensive had my role been so far, that I had not thought of the aggressive activity for which they begged. Experimentally, I reached out and opened the zip running along her inner elbow: a plump, white arm was revealed. I did not touch her at all, but stood well back and studied the other zips calculatingly, then tried the one which ran up from the ankle, above her black espadrilles. A shapely, smooth-shaven leg peeped out at me. I ran my fingers lightly over the bulge of the calf, and she shivered. Another pause. There were four zipped pockets on the front of the dress and, as I took her hand and turned her

50

gently round, I saw two more covering her plump arse. Curious, I opened one of these, only to find that the pocket was false, and there was soft flesh beneath. I slipped my hand in and felt her buttock, which was like satin, full, round and quivering under my caress. My right hand was soon in the other pocket, and I manipulated my two cornucopian handfuls elaborately and at length, while she writhed with pleasure.

My own excitement had redoubled. Taking out my hands, I slipped my cock inside one of the openings and, putting my arms round her from behind, felt for the vertical zips on the breast pockets, while I rubbed myself against her yielding arse. The upper zips were a good six inches long, affording me all the access I wanted. As soon as I had them open, and could feel long, heavy breasts inside, I knew exactly what I wanted to do with her. I pulled her left breast out through the unzipped opening, picked it up, dropped it, made it bounce up and down. I relished its weight in my hands, its innocent pliability. The right one I left inside, putting my hand in to caress it. As I toyed with her tits, the wide nipples became hard and swollen and I compressed them cruelly back against the surrounding flesh. Again and again they escaped and sprang erect, and I had to grasp them between my fingers, rotating them, then pulling them out, away from her body like elastic. Now she was moaning constantly with delight, and as my cock was rolled this way and that by the pressure of her buttocks I too felt myself on the point of dissolving in pleasure. But there were surprises to be savoured, zips still to be undone, so I moved right away from her, and resting my hand on the top of her head, I turned her round to face me again then made her sit on the edge of the bath.

Her face flushed with desire, she looked really beautiful now: mouth open, eyes narrowed and glinting black in the beams of light which bounced off the mirrors. First one, then the other, I opened her hip pockets and knelt in front of her, to force my hands down into the gaps. Her stomach was grossly distended by all the food, and must have been ultra-sensitive as a result, for I could feel it pulsing, and she cried out loud as my hands moved over it, exploring. Above this living mound, I could feel the indentation of her waist and, twisting my wrists to feel down below, I could tangle my fingers in the hair of her pudenda, but not quite reach her slit. But that could wait. Now I bent over her and put one hand behind on her buttocks, and one on her stomach, and kneaded and stroked these in slow harmony, making her gasp rhythmically, while I reached my mouth forward and suckled her heavy, flaccid breast greedily. But she had not resigned the active role entirely, to my relief, for she reached forward to take my prick, and held it tight in both hands as I moved in front of her. I knew I could make her come just by touching her huge belly, but then took care not to, as I remembered the final unopened zip, and what must lie beneath it. But still, this idyll of caresses seemed to continue for hours – we were both in a state of excitation which neither one would willingly destroy by a move or a pause for breath.

At last, my hunger became too sharp. Urgently, I ripped open the great zip that ran down the suit from throat to groin, and held the sides of the tunic apart to see the flawless and magnificent curves of her overfed flesh. Long olive breasts with dark brown nipples hung above the great globe of her stomach. Below that, in stark contrast, a thicket of stiff black hair, through which I glimpsed a hint of purple flesh. A further revelation, as I took her legs and moved them as wide apart as possible, so that she almost straddled the corner of the bath: there was a small zip under her crotch which joined the long one, making my future passage easy. This I undid in an instant, thrusting in a hand to discover that she was wet through and wide open. I made her stand up and lean back against the handbasin in her dismantled uniform, while I in my nakedness stood over her and penetrated her with long, deep strokes. Her cunt seemed to cling to me like suction rubber: I wanted to be swallowed up, and pushed in farther and farther. She could not move or even touch me because of the discomfort of her position, but she breathed quickly and heavily, and her eyes rolled this way and that, beyond control. I didn't fuck her for long – after such protracted preliminaries she was riper than the over-ripe mango. As she came she shrieked fiercely, and shook like an earthquake while I, needing nothing more to trigger me off, rammed deep down inside her, and poured myself out copiously.

After a Conversational Dinner

I dragged myself back to my room, even more drained
than I had been the last time and lay down again on my
bed. Immediately, there was a tap at the door and
Virginie walked in without waiting for my answer, to ask
if I wanted anything. I had no idea what *she* wanted, but
suspected that she had been watching closed-circuit
television. Rather churlishly, I asked her just to wake
me at seven, and turned over to sleep. I dozed lightly,
my dreams were a confused blur of mirrors, Florence's
food-stained face and mangoes bursting and squelching
over my body. I woke constantly in a state of sweaty
excitement, but finally fell into a deep, tranquil sleep
from which I was awoken by Virginie's knock. This time,
fortunately, she did not come in. I washed and dressed
with care, wishing to look composed when I met
Madame de Rochevillier and then walked across to the
house. The air was heavy with scented pollen, and the
French doors of the dining room which led on to the lawn

55

were open.

Madame was already waiting for me at the table, but she brushed aside my profuse apologies for my lateness and invited me to sit down. The first course, ham in aspic, was on the table, and I took some and started to eat ravenously. My share of the tempting lunch had, after all, been very small. Madame soon interrupted my silent chewing.

'So you enjoyed the Pyramus and Thisbe scene last night? A nice little mime, eh?'

Again, I was disconcerted by this frankness. I had grown accustomed to the idea that my movements were scanned by unseen watchers, and even welcomed the feeling that I was at the beck and call of the ladies of the house. These kinds of physical vulnerability seemed acceptable, but the fact that my actions were so freely commented on to my face was like total exposure. I had no defence against this verbal vulnerability.

'Thank you, yes. Julie seems to have a very idiosyncratic imagination.' I laughed inwardly as I stammered out this inane reply, but Madame laughed uproariously.

'You could say that. An analyst would say that she was neurotically obsessive in her desire to hide herself, especially as she has a lovely body. But that's the way she prefers it – *chacun à son goût*! More seriously, when I spoke to you yesterday, Monsieur, you said in passing something that worried me, something about research. I hope that you don't plan to put my little establishment in the newspapers? Of course, you gave me your word to maintain secrecy.'

I said that I had indeed, and had no intention of making any kind of exposé. To reassure her, I explained a little about my aspiration to write a scholarly account of women's sexual fantasies, adding that, if any material gathered there were used, it would be strictly anonymous and unlocated.

'How diligently you pursue your research,' she remarked mockingly. 'Such devotion to duty! However, the topic is particularly interesting. Although you define it as an academic problem, it is one that I have tried to solve here, at the practical level. Marriage may be an important institution but prostitution is equally important, and perhaps more permanent. There will always be men and women who need each other sexually outside the confines of socially or legally approved relationships, I'm certain, and money is a useful way of equating these needs. I do not talk only of female prostitution, you understand. The reason why that form predominates now is because of supply and demand, and the cultural norms which make man the free agent, the one with the cash.'

She spoke more convincingly on the subject than any sexologist or sociogist I had heard, and I begged her to go on.

'It is these same market forces that make men able to demand that prostitutes fulfil their fantasies. As you say, he who pays the piper calls the tune. In marriage, as out of it, this is true, as I know from experience. My two husbands – both men completely devoid of imagination – had domination fantasies of the most puerile kind, which I usually humoured because they did me no harm. But after thirty years of this charade, I began to think that they would really have enjoyed themselves more if *I* had set the scene and made them act. I knew that my own sexual caprices were far more vivid and varied than theirs would ever be. But by then it was too late: one was dead, one dying. And so, at the advanced age of fifty, I took a lover, a very gentle, young man, who said that he took almost more pleasure in acting out my fantasies than in fulfilling his own. What do you think of that? Would you say, as the world would, that made him less of a man?'

'Not at all,' I protested vehemently, defending myself as much as the unknown young man. 'Only if he effaced himself and his own desires to the point of becoming your abject slave, could that be said. To my mind, the affair with him that you describe is what normal sexual relationships might be in a less topsy-turvy world. Give-and-take, turn-and-turn-about, no dominating fantasy, but fantasies shared and exchanged.' I forced myself to add 'Maybe like my experience this afternoon.'

'Quite so. I'm not unaware that in speaking of my lover, I speak indirectly of you and the men like you who come here. Many people would say that because you wished to experience women's fantasies without dominating them, you were all masochists. How wrong they would be! Only in a perverse culture such as ours which puts such a premium on domination, activeness and sadism could anyone think that. It is our own corruption which decrees that complicity in a woman's desires denotes masochism or effeminacy.'

Cued perhaps by the word 'sadism', Virginie had appeared with a large roast, which she carved dexterously. For a time we both attended to the thick, rare beef. But the profundity of Madame's thoughts on the topic which so exercised me had fascinated me, and I broke the silence.

'Did you set up this institution in order to convert men

to this way of thinking, Madame?' Again, she laughed at my stilted delivery and replied robustly, 'Some hope!' She returned to her beef, but after some thought she spoke again.

'A brothel whose clientele is sworn to secrecy will make few converts. Only the already 'converted', to use your term, will ever find their way here. No, to be truthful, I set it up more for the sake of the women than the men. I thought that if I could save a dozen, two dozen, women from constant submission to the battering-ram of male fantasy, I would have increased the sum of human happiness by a few digits. If men like yourself can profit from this, so much the better, you deserve it. And of course,' she finished wryly, '*I* profit most of all!'

'But aren't most prostitutes so used to men's whims and wants that it's second nature to them? Can they ever re-accustom – or just accustom – themselves to giving free rein to their own desires?'

'That depends,' said Madame enigmatically.

'And how did you manage to find suitable women, with uncorrupted imaginations and genuinely 'female' fantasies?'

Another evasive answer: 'Advertising can work wonders.'

It was manifest that this particular line of questioning would get me nowhere. There was, I assumed, some murky secret about recruitment for the place which she would never reveal. But in any case, it seemed unimportant. So I asked the question that had besieged my brain for so long.

'I can see that you've been considering all this for even longer than I, so I must ask you this. What is it, do you think, that makes women's fantasy different – or even *better*?'

We had by now finished the meal, and Madame poured me a glass of armagnac from the decanter at her elbow, then offered me a cigar. I refused, but she lit one and relaxed back in her chair, drawing at it with deep contentment. She took her time answering me, and delivered her reply like a lecture.

'Freud says that penis envy forms and blights a woman's sexual life. If he is right, it would explain why we so willingly accept all the phallocentric myths and fantasies which men perpetrate. Maybe we even invent them, for some women worship the penis even more than men do themselves! I think there are better reasons why women go along with the cult of the phallus – the obvious one is that, in the right place at the right time, it affords incomparable pleasure. But Freud is right about one thing, that our dreams and fantasies are ultimately determined by our bodies, our basic physical attributes. If he had looked at what women *have* instead of what they lack, he might have allowed them some sexual identity of their own, and a unique fantasy life.

She took a deep breath, then went on. 'What special attributes have we got that make us different from men? Two round bumps and an extra orifice. These are the stuff of which dreams are made. Think about it, Monsieur Smith.'

I was mesmerised by her oracular manner and that fluent, foreign English, and would have listened to whatever wisdom or unwisdom she chose to expound for hours more, but her last sentence was undoubtedly a dismissal. She puffed at the cigar held between heavily-ringed fingers and seemed suddenly oblivious to my presence. So I stood up and thanked her for such a fascinating evening, and was bold enough to kiss her hand, a move which she approved by a gracious nod. Before I left, I asked if I was needed any more that evening, hoping that the answer would be no, so tired was I still.

'I imagine nobody has invited you upstairs tonight, so you are free to spend the rest of the evening in your room. Perhaps you will find something amusing on the television. Good night!'

I left through the French windows which were by now attracting a host of ghostlike moths that fluttered in the corona of light surrounding the fanlight above them. The evening was so pleasant that I sat under one of the willows near my building and contemplated the house and its mysteries. As usual, most of the upstairs windows were shuttered except for two on the first floor and one on the second. The first-floor windows were brightly lit, and I saw girlish shadows passing across them from time to time: I could faintly hear laughter and snatches of mournful jazz. The window above was actually open, and a woman was leaning out as if to breathe in the mixture of night rose and honeysuckle which pervaded the garden. In the rapidly falling darkness, I could not see her face, only the sheet of dark hair which hung round it. Julie, perhaps? I experienced a twinge of wistfulness at the memory, and even a hint of loneliness as I got up to go back to my room. How absurd to feel pangs about an unseen whore!

As I entered my suite, I was surprised to see a dim light coming from the bedroom. I went in and was greeted by the sight of a cello-shaped back such as Man Ray embellished in his notorious photograph, 'Le

Violon d'Ingres'. The naked girl, who was kneeling in front of the full-length mirror, looked up and addressed me in broken English. ''Allo. I am Danièle. I 'ave come to play with myself.' Taken aback, but vastly entertained by the idea, I sat down on the bed and regarded her minutely, examining her partly in the mirror as she was side-on to me. Her body was very promising, well-covered but shapely, with breasts which swelled outwards but showed no sign of drooping. Her kneeling position showed the long curve of her graceful back. Her face was haughty and aquiline, with piercing eyes and a thin mouth with a sensuous twist in it. Thick, club-cut brown hair hung to her shoulders, and she had a long, straight fringe. Bored with my silent gaze, she demanded petulantly 'You want watch me or television?'

'You, of course – please.'

Beside her stood an old-fashioned black bag, something like a Gladstone, into which she dipped, producing two squat candles, red and yellow, which she set down, one each side of her knees. She found matches and lit them. Unbidden I went and switched off the bedside lamp, then returned to my grandstand view. She was know covered with dancing shadows and bathed in a red glow from the candle on the side nearest to me: this light enhanced her lithe bodily movements, and made me feel I was watching a strange ritual of adoration or sacrifice. She tilted her head back and fixed her reflection with a steady gaze. Then she put her hands to her breasts and began to masturbate. I watched with fascination and even awe, for it was a sight seen by few initiates. Even men whose lovers will touch themselves up when they are in bed together have no idea of what a

62

woman will do alone: how she first arouses herself and finally brings herself off without the diversion of a man's presence. This girl first touched the tips of her nipples with the red nails of her two index fingers, scarcely moving and just scratching their surface. I saw these pink tips, which had formerly just been part of the undifferentiated curving contour of the breast, stiffen and stand out under this minimal stimulation, turning a dark rose colour. Then she brushed the palms of her hands symmetrically across the nipples with evident pleasure, for she lingered over this a long time. I could detect that her breasts were swelling already, reaching out, yearning to feel her hands. Now her hands covered her breasts, holding them and moving them up and down with slow deliberation. Her eyes were closed, her face smiling. She put the fingers of one hand round the left breast, forcing it to stand out further and shaking and moulding it into strange contortions, while her other hand toyed with its nipple.

As the silent magic continued, I could not resist undoing my trousers and handling my own, still tender, prick . . . but this pleasure was only secondary to my wonder at the vision in the corner. Forcing her breasts outward with her hands, she kneeled up and rubbed them against the mirror, exclaiming at its coldness. First the nipples touched, and then the whole breasts were pressed against it and she was writhing there, as if pinned to the mirror. In the distorted, flickering light, I fancied I was seeing two fabulous female Siamese twins with conjoined breasts, an impression which was strengthened when she kissed the mouth of her own reflection. Her state of arousal was manifest, and the excitement which she exuded infected me. As if exhausted by her narcissistic lovemaking, she sank back on her haunches, breathing hard, and reached into her bag again, bringing out a little pot of cream, which she spread over her nipples and smoothed slowly into the skin. How I itched to touch their silky texture at that moment – but a desire to see the final act kept me in my seat. Perhaps she would offer herself to me at the end? Her hands travelled downwards to her stomach and explored it casually, with the flat surface of her hands. Her eyes strayed from her face in the mirror to her stomach and back distractedly, and her face had a faraway expression.

She curved her back further, to make her stomach more prominent and for a few moments offered me the extraordinary silhouette of a girl a few months pregnant before she stopped her caresses, straightened up and got to her feet.

'Help me please.'

She beckoned me over. The mirror was fixed to the door of a fitted cupboard which opened against the wall. She stood in the corner, back to the wall, and made signs to me to open the door and press the mirror against her. I did so reluctantly because it obscured my view of her, but by looking round the edge of the door I could see her, very close, head back, breasts and stomach thrown forward and flattened against the door, and her mouth opened in a silent 'Oh' of pleasure.

'Harder, please.'

I obliged until she said 'Enough', and emerged again from her impromptu body press. My brief role as sorcerer's apprentice was evidently ended, and I returned to my bed and watched. Kneeling down once more, she briefly stroked her excited breasts and then plunged her hands down between her legs. At first I could see nothing of how she performed this most secret part of the rite but then, as if to please me, although I'm sure that it was her usual custom, she lay back flat on the floor, legs drawn up to her hips. The mirror and candles were so positioned to afford me a perfect view of her hands playing with her neat, pretty cunt.

One hand held the labia apart, while she ran her fingers up and down the soft, exposed membranes, with a light touch. The men who imagine that pressure, or even roughness, in those parts is the way to a girl's orgasm, should have seen the delicacy with which Danièle touched her clitoris, and blended gentleness with total excitation. Once she spat saliva into her hand and smoothed it over the folds of flesh. The ritual was a silent one, though I saw her shuddering and catching her breath as she pleased herself more and more. Then she called to me 'Come over, please,' and sat up to reach once more in her bag. She pulled out a great black dildo, moulded like a prick. Its designer had, I thought, been carried away by phallocentric mythology when he decided on its dimensions. But she thrust it at me, and made it clear that I was to officiate again at that last stage of the spell when the magician himself is busy disappearing in a cloud of smoke. As she lay back again and closed her eyes, I was tempted to substitute my own instrument for the crude plastic thing. But if she was attuned to this inflexible, ten-inch wizard, she would instantly notice a human surrogate and surely be furious.

The dildo in my right hand, I opened her cunt's lips with my left, and gingerly inserted it inch by inch into the hole which at first seemed so soft and tiny that I thought it would reject even the tip of the adamant monster.

Although she winced as I introduced it, the flesh yielded and the passage expanded and finally the dildo's whole length had disappeared into her. The girl was still caressing her stomach; she opened her eyes to say 'Move, please.' As the dildo came out, I saw it was wet with her juice, and soon it slipped in and out as if greased.

Much as I hated my confinement to the humble role of machine operator, and longed to touch her body, I did not even brush against her curving thigh, but kept my hands demurely in the gap between her legs. As I worked the dildo in and out I sensed that even the merest touch would have destroyed the autonomy of her fantasy although I was an acceptable accomplice while separated from her by the length of black plastic. We must have appeared a strange couple, two rhythmically moving bodies whose pivotal axis was a small plastic rod. But my back was to the mirror, so I could not enjoy the sight. I tried it slow, I tried it fast, but she seemed to prefer the tentative, tantalising approach. Momentarily, I felt a disembodied power over her, more total and complete than if it had been *my* cock in her cunt. I was the master of the tool which was the master of her pleasure. The tool had no will of its own, and if I stopped – I did this for a minute experimentally, and she called out hoarsely 'More!' – she was marooned. Yet I had no temptation to exploit this power, and was bent on giving her satisfaction.

As my mind wandered around the idea of the dildo, I remembered that the prick of a pig resembles a corkscrew, and I hit upon a new technique of twisting the dildo as I pushed it in. I grudgingly admitted to myself that the artefact was more versatile than its human original, which could never emulate the pig's screwing like this. The new sensation delighted Danièle, who wriggled ecstatically and begged me to continue whenever I showed any sign of pausing. In this way, as my magic wand corkscrewed into and through her most secret nerve centres, I brought her right to the edge of orgasm, and saw her stomach flush rose pink. Then one last push, up to the hilt, and she broke her long silence and began to cry out, long low cries of deep, delayed satisfaction.

Afterwards she remained flat on the floor, her eyes closed. The altruist in me felt that I too had come, and I buttoned my trousers and lay back on the bed, enjoying the sight of her fulfilled body splayed out on the floor in the uncertain candlelight. A few minutes later, Danièle sat up and started to pack. I put on the light and she blew out the candles, put them into her bag, fastened it and stood up to go, saying, 'Merci beaucoup.' Still we had not touched. I escorted her to the door of the building and was rewarded by the sight of a naked girl carrying a Gladstone bag picking her way across the silver lawn in the light of a full moon.

I lay awake for a long time, pondering on this haunting episode. Its cinematic and ritualistic qualities removed it from the other fantasies that I had experienced here, and placed it in a category transcending the merely sexual, the category of the beautiful. And yet it had been a supremely exciting experience. The truth was that though I had not come, and had been erect all the time she was in the room, I did not now feel frustrated. Had my satisfaction been entirely vicarious, or in another dimension? And could it be that women on their own elevate their auto-sexuality to an aesthetic level which they can never attain in the corrupting presence of men? Searching for answers, I fell soundly asleep.

Next day I woke early and was shaved and dressed before Virginie erupted into the room with my breakfast, without knocking at all. She looked vaguely disappointed not to find me still in bed, but placed my breakfast on a table by the open window, and started to make the bed. The last two days had so expanded my conceptions of sexual provocation and pleasure that the last thing I now thought of was rolling on the unmade bed with the maid, even though she had exchanged her severe straight skirt for a dramatically short mini-skirt, which became her long legs very well. But I was sure that my cruder appetite would return in time, and I would find out whether or not her lascivious demeanour hid a puritanical soul. She gave me to understand that lunch would be brought to my room and that I was expected in 'Room 14' after lunch. She explained how to find it, saying pointedly that it was her afternoon off; she also showed me how to work the television set, which received the usual public channels, but had a special switch for the closed-circuit broadcasts. I asked whether they were live or recorded transmissions and was told some sets (among them, no doubt, Madame's and her own) showed them live, but that this set would show a variety of recorded excerpts, so that I must switch on and take pot luck. I resolved to try it out very soon.

I settled down to eat, gazing at the garden. It was a glorious morning and, when I had finished, I carried out my chair and my notebooks and sat in in my shirt-sleeves in the sun to make some notes towards my *magnum opus*. It seemed too soon to attempt a coherent account

68

or synthesis, so I decided to write a few paragraphs under any headings that occurred to me. As I reconsidered and tried to analyse the evening that I arrived, the first heading was obvious.

ORIFICES: Holes, apertures and openings always seem to be a major theme in women's fantasy, no doubt because their genitals take this form themselves. (Here I mentally thanked Madame de Rochevillier for the lead that she had given me last night over dinner.) Inserting their own most protuberant parts, such as breasts, through some suitable aperture (here I had flashbacks to Julie's nipple in the wall, and Florence's breast thrusting through her zip pocket) is a cause of sexual excitement which may be increased if a man is involved in the erotic activity, and can draw or push their breasts through the orifice. The fact that the orifice plays a central part makes women's fantasy resemble that of men, but only superficially, since male sexuality concentrates on the act of *penetration*, while the woman seeks escape *out of* the orifice.

When I re-read this, it seemed rather slick and in need of certain subtle qualifications, so I added:

One could, however, say that it is the orifice itself which is the focus of women's attention, not the activity, as they seem indifferent as to whether something is extruded or intruded through the orifice. (I thought of Florence's excitement as I inserted my hands in between her zips). In the case of their own genitals, of course, intrusion is the only possibility, but women, as is well-known, fantasise about inserting a large variety of objects, as well as the penis, into their sexual orifice. As a result of this orificial orientation (here I congratulated myself on my scientific prose) the enactment of women's fantasies frequently involves the creation of apertures or orifices through which some form of extrusion can take place.

All this seemed respectably scholarly and abstract, but too removed from the graphic reality which I had witnessed. My attention wandered and was caught by Virginie walking across from the big house to the outhouses with a mop and a pail. I had never seen her doing any form of cleaning, and indeed I very much doubted that her skintight clothes would allow the necessary bending. And would she really start cleaning on Sunday? I had the uncanny feeling that her appearance was planned for my benefit and that it, like everything else here, was part of a backdrop in front of which a burlesque was being played for the diversion of one solitary spectator, myself. But the warm sun was soothing, and I forgot this disturbing insight, and closed my eyes. I could hear the bees above my head, and the faintest suggestion of church bells borne on the wind, not from the godless village but from a distant town.

Crunching footsteps on the gravel made my eyes open with a start, in time to see a woman approaching down the drive from the road, carrying a suitcase. She was about twenty-five, with wavy golden hair fit for a forties film-star and an exquisitely pretty, piquant face. Her dress was very smart in a thoroughly bourgeois way – a white, tailored cotton suit under a matching swagger coat, caught together at the throat with a brooch – and the impression of wealth was reinforced by the large pigskin suitcase. She paused as she reached the lawn: her glance passed over and through me, and she turned left towards the big house and disappeared inside. I was disturbed by the attractive new arrival and wondered when I might be invited to her room. But then, ashamed of my laziness, I addressed myself again to my notebook.

TUMESCENCE: Many people believe that this is the male prerogative, because of the remarkable tumescent powers of the penis, but the woman's genitals and her nipples have the same property, though to a less dramatic degree. What differentiates women from men is that, as well as inducing and enjoying tumescence in these areas, they try to create artificial tumescence by making the already protuberant parts of their bodies more prominent. Both the *process* of tumescence and the *result* of protuberance are integral ingredients of their fantasy. Thus, a woman will handle her breasts in such a way as to make them protrude further: the now defunct brassiere fulfilled the same function, although its manifest purpose was decency and health. A woman will also thrust out her stomach, or eat to swell it, as this makes it more sensitive. Here there is a clear analogy with pregnancy, which is in a sense the original induced tumescence in both breasts and stomach. However, the origin is relatively unimportant, for in sexual fantasy and dream life, bodily objects such as the swollen stomach take on a symbolic role in themselves and their pleasure

71

quotient attaches to this, and not to any function or purpose that they might have in daily life.

I felt that I was beginning to master the analytical side of the subject. What would be harder would be to use my empirical data to prove conclusively the truth of these abstractions. A further perception occurred to me as I read over what I had written, and I added a few more sentences, headed 'The Puerility at the Root of Fantasy'.

The orifice and tumescence, which bulk so large in the fantasies of both sexes are, it will be remarked, the very features which fascinate the sexually undifferentiated infant from the earliest age. He seeks to introduce his fingers or fists into apertures and to take hold of anything protuberant such as the breast, and including his own genitals, which the older male child soon learns to make tumescent. This phenomenon is cited here, not to justify the psychoanalysts who make childhood the sole and determining basis for the adult's conscious and subconscious life, but to point out that the construction of a fully satisfying male or female fantasy is bound to include somewhere these two components.

At this point I suspected after all that I had not entirely mastered the subject, and decided to call it a day. Going inside, I switched on the television, tuning in to the private circuit. Obviously the fixed camera system had the great disadvantage that its pictures were not always in focus, and the first few shots were so blurred that I could make nothing out. Then the picture resolved itself into a clear one of two women sitting together on an ottoman fully clothed. One had short, dark hair and the other, long, fairish hair, and both had the style of dress and make-up typical of movies of the early twenties, imitated to perfection. A man in a striped blazer came jerkily into view, and they made him sit down between them, each taking one of his hands. Then they turned towards him, almost obscuring him from the camera, which pointed straight at the group, and while one removed his tie and began to undo his shirt, the other tugged impatiently at his belt and unbuttoned his wide flannel trousers. This silent mime had a threatening quality. When the unbuttoning was complete, the fair one pulled off his shirt and jacket while the other took off his shoes, then his trousers. During all this, all three faces remained perfectly impassive. The girls then stood up and arranged him on the sofa, lying down.

The dark girl disappeared and came back with a lighted cigarette in an exaggeratedly long holder and sat down on the floor by the man's head. From behind the sofa the other produced a short whip with a cluster of thongs, which appeared to be rope rather than leather. While her friend watched approvingly, she drew these over the length of his body, starting at the feet. From his sudden movements I could guess the ticklishness of this process. The dark girl meanwhile blew clouds of smoke into his face. Then she took his hands and held them behind his head while her partner began to whip his stomach and chest. The tangible silence made it impossible to judge what force she was using, but I saw his body move spasmodically from side to side as if in pain while, paradoxically, his cock rose into view and remained vertical. Ash from the long cigarette fell on his chest and made him wince.

The picture flickered for a few seconds and, when it had righted itself, the brunette was sitting squarely on the unfortunate's chest, still pinioning his arms while the other came back into the picture, her whip discarded, drawing on a pair of black shiny gloves which reached to her uncovered elbow. Standing between his legs, which hung over the end of the ottoman, she seized his sex and began to masturbate it rapidly. For a second, the girls smiled at each other in complicity: they reminded me of nothing more than two vultures. The finale was his ejaculation – here, I suspected trick photography, for it spouted in a great arc, drenching the dark girl's dress, for which she uncharitably slapped his face as he lay there impotently. The tableau faded and I was surprised to see credits appearing, and the trademark of some long-forgotten film company, 'Eros Films Inc.'. One of the earliest blue movies!

The videotape evidently broadcast continuously because the next episode appeared immediately. Now we were in the present, and I instantly recognised myself, stark naked and viewed from above, lying on Florence's dining table as on a butcher's marble slab. The film of Florence's meal was interesting largely because of the unusual angle of the shots (I concluded that the camera had been concealed in the branching light fixture above the table) and the idiotic smile which I had been quite unaware of wearing during the proceedings. The backroom boys, or girls, were certainly good editors, for careful cutting had reduced our protracted pantomime to some twenty, action-packed minutes. My narcissism was nourished by the shots in the bathroom –

my lean body endlessly reflected, rampantly erect, seemed to tower over and menace soft, plump Florence as I delved into the secret openings of her costume.

When our scene reached its dramatic *dénouement*, I switched off, my imagination pleasantly satiated. On the chest of drawers near the sitting-room door was a lunch-tray which I had not previously noticed, so I sat down to eat. I was thoughtful. The regular but hidden clockwork of the house still mystified me: I had seen no signs at all of cooking, and could not even guess where this took place, or who was the chef. Yet the food was always excellent and my tray was laden with cold meat, fish, fruit and a good bottle of Beaujolais. Likewise with the television apparatus: where was the master screen, who did the editing, and how? And, most mysterious of all, where were all the whores and how did they occupy themselves when not on call? The only woman apart from Madame and Virginie that I had seen outside a bedroom was the beauty who had arrived that morning. The films that I had just seen also preyed on my thoughts. The first one annoyingly eluded the categorisation of fantasy which I had laboriously invented, since it seemed to represent a fantasy genuinely shared by both sexes: subjugation and rape by two women excited and appealed enormously to me, yet I intuited that the inscrutable actresses had enjoyed their role as well. Perhaps sado-masochism obliterated the male–female distinction and the roles were reversible: man or woman could play either part with equal ease. Yet I was convinced that women are habitually less sadistic than men for, even in my passive role here, what I had experienced was tantalising, mysterious or playful, never cruel. Suddenly I saw that it was two o'clock, and with a new surge of energy I set off to find Room 14.

The Room Without a View

My route took me up the servants' stairs to the top of the house, where the decor was less opulent than on the first floor. The corridor was bare and white and uncarpeted, and I passed several plain wooden doors before coming to one which bore the number 14. When I knocked, it opened a few inches and a hand poked round it, holding out a brown silk scarf. A woman's voice asked me to blindfold myself. More games, I thought irritably, but, being in a good humour, I tied the scarf round my eyes as tightly as I could manage. I heard the door open wider and a hand took mine, and pulled me inside, turning me round several times like the stooge in Blind Man's Buff. In the absence of sight and touch, my other senses worked overtime. There was a faint, sweet smell tinged with lemon – perfume, I supposed – and I thought I could detect the warmth of a body nearby, and the sound of light breathing. For at least a minute nothing happened, then hands reached over my shoulders from behind and wandered over my face and throat, slowly moving down inside my open-necked shirt. Cool, light fingers traced the line of my collar bones and the arch of the armpit as if lost and uncertain of their direction. The blind feeling the blind? My shirt was opened and the fingers returned to explore the muscles of my chest, a journey terminating at my nipples, which seemed to fascinate the hands, so long did they spend experimentally pinching and pressing them like bell-pushes.

Then the hands were down below, sliding over my stomach and creeping down into my trousers insidiously, as far as their tightness would allow. It was not a massage, it was a primal, instinctive exploration of one body by another, as blind kittens nuzzle each other. But this was still unilateral – my hands hung stiffly at my sides. But as her hands divested me of my trousers, my abdomen seemed to lurch with desire. The hands were back now, running up my thighs, round the groin, delicately avoiding my cock which nevertheless sensed their nearness and began to grow big. The blindfold now annoyed me, despite the thrilling sensation which the unexpected hands gave me, as I wanted to see their owners, but I dared not move or protest. When finally they pulled off my shirt, the soft voice exclaimed 'Yes, you really *are* sexy!' Then someone fumbled with the knot of the scarf, and suddenly I was sighted again.

So dimly lit was the room I was in that my eyes saw little at first. The room had no window and there was some sort of plush on the walls, dark maroon in colour. The sole source of light was an opaque globe on the floor in a corner, with a very small, yellow bulb inside. Much of the floor was taken up by a low bed on which bright cushions and fur rugs were scattered in disarray. I was startled by the only other decoration in the room – two hideous devils with curved horns and bulging eyes mocked me from the wall where the window should have been. Japanese theatre masks with their awful, equivocally grinning or snarling teeth, as garish and fearful now as at the time of their manufacture, centuries ago. Their eyes glowed faintly red from a light concealed behind them. Meanwhile, my captor stood behind me, her soft hands encircling my waist and caressing my stomach.

'You can turn round now,' she said.

I turned and was shocked again – I was looking into the fierce face of a cat! The mask was made of black feathers, expertly arranged to represent feline features, and through the eyeholes, green, catlike eyes stared back at me. Beneath her mask the girl was naked. Her tall, boyish figure emerged almost naturally below her cat's face: straight hips, and hardly a hint of a waist. Her breasts were so tiny that she might have been a young catamite running to fat there, but when I looked down, this was no longer a boy. A round black bush spread out over the mound between her thighs, reflecting the black of her mask. Her shoulders were broader than her hips warranted, but elegantly sculptured, and her buttocks small, tight and high.

Her sexual ambiguity delighted me and I longed to inflict all manner of perversions on this inscrutable boy-girl. She seemed passive and recipient, a true catamite, so I took her buttocks in my hands and worked them apart. Never had an arse-hole looked so succulent. It beckoned my cock at once, but I wanted to delay this pleasure, so I pressed myself against her back, and ran my fingers down the front of her body. Her skin had a wonderful firm, smooth texture and was slightly damp with sweat. I could smell her raw armpits, mingled with that piquant, citrus scent. The miniature breasts scarcely impeded the movement of my hands, yet as they passed over, I could feel them tightening, stirring. The nipples, so formless and masculine, seemed to take shape as my hands returned upwards. Yet I could not treat them like a woman's tits, but rubbed my hands over them casually, as I do over my own nipples, until I felt her draw in her breath sharply. Then I made her bend down, forwards, and stood over her. She was just the right height for what I had in mind, and I was able to press my prick against her buttocks without even bending my legs.

Unhurriedly, I took it in one hand and pressed the tip against that inviting hole at the centre of her arse, teasing it round and round, making feints at entering her, which made her shiver with anticipation. Already I was lubricating so freely that there was no need for spit, or cream, and I knew I could just go in when I was ready. So, pulling the round cheeks wide apart, I made my entry. The first inch is never easy, but my cock was hard as a ramrod and drove itself in without help from my hands, which were busy manhandling her buttocks, forcing them away from each other, to ease my passage. As I penetrated deeper, I had that unique sensation of imprisonment. I was held in a vicelike grip which squeezed all the harder as my excitement mounted. Fully inside at last, I was able to move a little, from side to side, then in and out by slow degrees. She had made no noise as I entered her but now, with each assault and retreat, she cried out in a voice somewhere between pain and pleasure – I still wonder which. Now I was ready for an orgy, and I buggered her freely and almost uncontrollably until I thought I would die of pleasure. Under this sharp, relentless stimulus, she abandoned herself and came again and again as I thrust wildly, now hugging her hips tightly, now taking hold of her splayed white buttocks to press them closer together and make the tabooed channel even harder to navigate. Her climaxes, one after another, thrilled me unbearably, but I could not stop or come, so great was my joy in eating this forbidden fruit. When in a strangled voice she called out to me to stop, I was pouring with sweat and so transported by my own momentum that I took ages slowing down and coming out of her.

She fell forwards on to the bed, face down, and I did likewise, feeling I might never move again. Perhaps we had been there a quarter of an hour when I heard her get up and go into another room, which I did not know existed. When she came back, she offered me a glass of ice cold fruit juice which revived me and dispelled my exhaustion. But we lay there still, stroking each other like lovers, and I memorised the contours of her unfeminine body, taking pleasure in the flatness of her belly, and in provoking her non-existent breasts until the nipples budded. I sucked those milkless buds until she arrived again at the point of orgasm and said I must please stop, it was too soon. Her mask still taunted me with its feline sensuality, but despite my longing to pull it off and see her entirely, I left her face covered. Since I could not kiss her mouth, I contented myself with kissing her body from the throat downwards until I reached her other pussy. I was almost at a loss what to do there, for I still ached to be inside her arse again. Could that other passage ever grip so firmly, or suck my sperm out of me so voraciously?

But she opened her legs and made signs that I should touch her there, so with one hand I stretched back the skin on her mound of Venus, pulling tight the long mouth of her cunt, while the other fondled her there, playing at sealing the lips together, then coaxing them apart. Another surprise awaited me here, for when I felt inside the moist lips, her clitoris was huge and elongated. I thought of that celebrated mythical creature, the hermaphrodite, and wondered whether this girl was really a sexual hybrid with a vestigial penis and perfect cunt. So swollen and sensitive was her organ that when I bent down to kiss and play with it, she begged me not to touch it since the slightest sensation was '*insupportable*'.

Then she made me lie down on my back again, and put her cunt over my mouth, smothering my cock with her feathery face which tickled me wickedly, and stroking it with her hands, while my tongue made its way into her cunt and drank the salty liquor which it found there. She worked on my cock until it stood vertical, and then wrapped it round with my silk blindfold which lay on the floor near the bed, so that it looked like a bandaged sore thumb, with just the tip visible, and the puckered hole in the foreskin. She titillated this tiny protuberance with her tongue, then eased back the skin inch by inch to gnaw and suck at the wet, bulging bulb inside, while I lay back helpless, drunk with the sensation. The bandaging scarf, like a tourniquet, made me immobile and rigid, even against my will. My cock seemed protected, yet was totally vulnerable to the depredations of her hungry mouth. It seemed detached from me, no longer my instrument, but her toy. Finally, her tongue brought me to such a pitch of frenzy that I pushed her off me and rolled over, hands over my balls to shield myself from further delight. When I was calmer, the cat-girl bent over and unwrapped my tender, pulsing member, then sat cross-legged at the end of the bed, demurely stroking my ankles and feet, while I rested my head on a cushion and admired her strange body, and marvelled at the long tongue of pink flesh protruding beneath her pubic hair. All was a dark blur in this windowless room except her pale limbs and astonishing cat's face. Time passed; I was in a limbo of pleasure, and even felt love for the face I could not see.

Perhaps she thought that I had been silent and inactive for too long, because she took one hand from my leg and started to caress herself, and as the pink ribbon of flesh between her legs grew thicker and more prominent it attracted my cock magnetically. I felt new lust and sat up, reaching out my arms to her, but she got up and went over to the wall, where she took down one of the atrocious masks, revealing a dull red light behind. She told me to put it on, which was not too difficult as there was a strong band of elastic attached to the sides. But it was made of a very solid kind of plaster and I was insufferably hot inside it, and weighed down by it. I realised how uncomfortable her feather mask must have been for the past hours, and thought how devoted she must be to the cause of her fantasy to tolerate such discomfort. In the meantime, the girl had opened the door of a fitted cupboard, which had a long mirror fixed inside it, and swung it back flush to the wall. She brought me over to look at myself and the sight was truly diabolical. A grinning, glaring demon's face surmounted my body, made red by the light, which looked ready for some infernal debauch, with its satanic, rearing phallus;

beside me, that delicate androgynous body and expressionless pussy-cat face which so provoked me. Our behaviour is surely determined by the masks we wear, even in normal life. I was seized by the urge for demonic rape, and pulled her back to the bed, where I threw myself on top of her, pushing my mask against hers, grinning teeth against whiskers, while I plunged my devil's prick into her and fucked her as crudely as I knew how.

I forgot myself and became the devil, and she his familiar. No finesse now, the rougher and more rending my movements, the better I was pleased. I wanted to defile her, to tear apart that enigmatic body and drag out its secrets. But I pleased her too and she gasped 'More! You arse-licking devil, fuck me to hell!', while I could feel her clitoris reaching out like a moth's long proboscis and rubbing against my prick as it slid in and out. As soon as this exquisite friction started, I felt her body burning against mine, and shaking, and she came almost at once, screaming this time. But the devil in me had not violated enough, and I gave her no time to recover from this onslaught, but pulled her up off the bed. I dragged her to the mirror, and forced her shoulders down, and lifted her buttocks with my hands. Maybe she was unwilling, maybe she faked unwillingness, but now it was so hard to penetrate her that I had to use my hands to enlarge her closed-up hole, and push myself in, and she groaned at this new violation. The devil grinned back at me from the mirror, daring me to greater vileness, and I battered away savagely at my fallen angel, all my lust distilled into my vessel which pierced her small, tight arse-hole – until, suddenly, it spilled out in a moment of frantic, fiendish joy. Nor had my devilry subdued the whore because as I came and my thrusting began to subside, I heard again her unearthly, orgasmic screams.

Shattered as I was, I managed to tear off the spell-binding, suffocating mask before I fell on the bed and lay as if paralysed. Now that the demon had been exorcised, I felt extremely penitent, in case I had hurt the frail androgyne. She lay beside me, still as death, and I put my arms round her and held her tight, while the feathers of her mask tickled my face and nose. Perhaps her eyes were shut behind her mask, I could not tell, but for a few minutes we rested like this and romantic thoughts washed over my mind, which I was feeling too feeble to banish. I started to stroke her again, but she said 'You must go now. Dinner will be very soon.' Admonished, I got up and dressed hastily. With a long, devouring look at the haunting catgirl on the bed, I slipped out, closing the door softly. When I was back in my room, I saw that she had deceived me – or exaggerated – to get rid of me, I supposed, since it was not yet six o'clock. Feeling not like a devil of a fellow, but like a sponge which had been wrung very dry, I lay down for the early evening sleep that had become almost a habit in this tiring household.

Bawdy Tales

Nobody was in the dining room when I entered through the open windows, so I examined the three framed prints which hung together on one wall. They proved to be some of the nastier sketches of Goya. Witches or old crones with withered paps loomed large in the first and the second was a carnival scene with evil masks. With a start, I recognised myself in the third: a gleeful devil intent on sodomy, it seemed, with a young cherub. I found this representation strangely repellant and moved away hastily, just as Madame came into the room carrying a tray with three glasses and a bottle of champagne sweating with cold. She must have noticed me looking at the pictures because she said pointedly 'Goya has a talent for portraying the true debauchery of our inner selves, don't you agree?' I could do nothing else! Then, 'We have another eating companion tonight, so let's have a glass of champagne to celebrate. Will you open the bottle, please?'

While I did this, Madame poured a quantity of angostura bitters into her own glass to make what is usually called 'pink champagne'. I declined this, having been brought up to believe that it was the vulgarest of drinks, but she explained that she had a distaste for any trace of sugar in alcohol, and that bitters took away the faint sweetness of this Kremer. 'I hope that your Sunday has passed profitably,' she said. 'I saw you doing a prodigious amount of writing this morning on the lawn.'

I said that on the contrary I was distressed by the slowness of my thoughts on the subject which absorbed me, and that I hoped to have the pleasure of hearing more of her views on women's sexuality very soon.

'Nothing would please me more,' she replied. 'It is rare to have such an attentive and sympathetic listener. But this evening you will hear the opposite point of view. Madame Chantal, who is joining us, will give you her observations on male fantasy, on which she is something of a specialist.'

'How is that, Madame? Is she a psychoanalyst?'

Madame gave her infectious, fruity laugh. 'One of nature's psychoanalysts, you might say! In fact, she spent some time working in a *bordel* in the South of France which was quite the reverse of my establishment. This was a brothel exclusively catering for the desires of very rich male clients. Chantal could not –'. Here she broke off, hearing a footfall, and went to greet the other guest.

I had a sudden sense of *déjà-vu* and when I saw Chantal in the doorway. There was the same straight, slim body that I had so abused that afternoon. Her slender legs were clad in black, skintight satin trousers, tucked into boots and she wore a close-fitting velvet jacket, with a strip of lace knotted at the neck. The face whose concealment had pained and provoked me then was at last revealed, delicate and still remarkably catlike. Her green eyes were very large indeed, almost eclipsing the rest of her fragile, angular boy's face. The sleek black hair was brushed back behind her ears, enhancing her feline appearance, although strands of it escaped over her temples and forehead. Madame de Rochevillier introduced her to me with great formality, and she put her familiar hand in mine as though for the first time. I was so thrilled to meet that creature of dreams in her daytime incarnation that I sat down at the table without ever taking my eyes off her.

In the absence of Virginie and the cook, the table was set with a cold buffet from which we served ourselves. Chantal apparently understood no English, so we slipped back into French and exchanged pleasantries about the state of the world as we settled down to eat. Then Madame spoke to Chantal.

'As you know, Monsieur Smith is studying the sexual fantasy of women, and I thought that you could regale him with some stories of male fantasy, for the purposes of comparison.'

'Why, certainly!' answered Chantal, and addressed herself to me without hesitation. Perhaps she had already been cued. 'My experiences were maybe not of the happiest kind, nor the most representative of what men fantasise, owing to the peculiarities of my clients, who were elderly, jaded and very rich. But perhaps in one sense they were typical of the male ideal of dominance through money, for these men thought they could buy anything in a skirt. They would approach perfectly respectable women in the streets of Cannes, and offer them fabulous sums of money to spend a day or two in the brothel. I suppose that forms the framework of many men's fantasies – to buy whoever they want, completely, like a slave.'

'Did these women ever accept?' I asked.

'I know that some of them accepted,' she replied, 'for I was one of those who did. A man of about sixty-five, something like a retired banker, approached me when I was sitting in a café on the main street. His proposition interested me because, although I was not short of money, I thought the experience might be exciting. So he gave me the address of the place and said he would visit me there the next morning. When I arrived, it was a small hotel, devoted entirely to this kind of part-time prostitution, and run by a mercenary woman who explained that she would take fifty per cent of whatever he paid me. In return for this, I would get board and lodging, and I would have the use of any "equipment" that my client might require. She clearly knew all the clients and their obsessions far better than the women whom they lured there.'

I caught Madame smiling to herself, and guessed that her business worked on similar principles.

'I had dinner there that evening and talked to some of the women who had been there before, who told me horrifying stories of flagellation and mortification, and of practices which seemed unnatural even to me, although I was well-versed in the ways of this particular world. So I awaited my client with great trepidation the next day. But when he arrived, he looked harmless enough. He brought with him a huge box of cigars which he smoked constantly, and a case full of dressing-up clothes.'

'For himself?' I interrupted.

'At first, they all seemed to be for me. I had to dress as a bathing beauty, and parade around the room in high heels and a swimming costume, which didn't suit my figure at all! He had a whip with him, and cracked it like a ring-master to make me turn round or move in a certain way. If I misunderstood him he would send it curling round my legs, which hurt and made me very angry, though I didn't show it. But at least he did not move from his armchair, or try to touch me. Then, I had to dress as a maid and serve him drinks from the fridge in the room, while he pinched my bottom or stuck his hand up my skirt. I didn't especially mind that – it was child's play beside the humiliations of generations of maid-servants! But then I had to get into a nurse's uniform, with a starched apron, but very *décolleté*. He complained that he had a pain in his penis (which he called "my little willy") and said I must examine him. So I undid his zip and poked around with various instruments that he gave me (how I wished they had been scalpels!) while he tried to put his hand down the front of my dress, pretending all the time to be an invalid who didn't quite know what he was doing.'

'Would it be impertinent to ask, Madame Chantal,' I interrupted again. 'Whether you found this masquerade in the slightest degree *exciting*? It is an important point, because I am trying to discover whether women are ever moved by men's fantasies – as *I* certainly am by women's – or whether they are always just a gratuitous imposition.'

'*Excited*?' repeated Chantal with vitriolic scorn, and laughed. 'I despised and was repelled by the posturings this man forced me to go through. Most of all, I knew that it was his intention to humiliate me, and humiliation is only exciting if, like men, you are accustomed to dominate. If he could not humiliate women in public, he thought he could buy their dignity and destroy it in private. It became clear that this was his purpose, because *he* then undressed and put on an army uniform which was also in his case. I think he fancied himself a Brigadier-General – it was covered with brass and medals and made him look like a performing monkey. Then he told me to look in a cupboard in the corner – clearly, he had used the room many times before – and bring out what I found there. It was a bayonet. He made me take off the nurse's dress and then *drill* – naked except for my stiletto shoes, with my back to him – while he shouted orders. Whenever I went wrong, which was often, he would prick my bum with the point of his bayonet, or slap the blade across my thighs. I was terrified of being slashed, but the more I tried to obey his commands, the more he jabbed at me. He made me turn round and march on the spot in front of him, while he came close and felt my breasts, or stood back and poked the bayonet into my pubic hair.'

'Was that the end of the performance?' I asked.

'No, the final mortification was that I had to lie on the bed while he whipped me with all his strength, which luckily was not very great. I could endure that better – at least it was straightforward sadism! And then, worn out, he flopped on top of me and masturbated until he came all over my arse. I was nauseated; I wanted to impale his balls on his bayonet. Then he washed off his own filth, dressed, packed, put five thousand francs on the pillow, and left without a word. I never saw him again, thank God!'

I observed Madame, to see how she was affected by this risqué narrative, but she was serenely picking her way through a cold salmon, and made no comment when it ended. Chantal had eaten nothing while she talked, and I very little as I listened, so we now set about the fish, and I meditated on the significance of her story. It could have been pure invention, so neatly did it caricature the blend of sexism, sadism, and status and power consciousness that pervades the sexual dreams of many men – but I sensed that it was a true history. I asked her whether she had ever had any contrary experiences where the man chose to be humiliated. She gave a very intelligent reply:

'Yes, but the point is, he still *chooses*, because he pays. So how can it be true humiliation?'

'I don't know,' I admitted.

'Well, I'll tell you what happened, then you can judge. After this client had left, I complained bitterly to the brothel-keeper as she took my hard-earned money. But she clearly wanted to keep me in her service for a few days, as a new, tasty piece of merchandise, so she promised that if I stayed there she would send me a very undemanding gentleman who would want *me* to dominate *him*. He would pay even better, and she would take only forty per cent this time. I was moved to another bedroom with a strange piece of equipment like a very large high-chair, and that evening the 'gentleman' arrived. He was younger than the other one, about fifty-five, with a strong physique, not bad-looking. He wore shorts, and at first I thought he had just come from the beach. But this was his costume. He sat in the high-chair and wanted to be treated like a little boy. I had to feed him with a spoon from a bowl with Martini in it, then

93

force him to smoke cigarettes, holding them between my fingers. He didn't want to touch me at all, but kept calling me "Mummy". And I had to keep talking the whole time, praising him as a "good boy" when he swallowed his drink or smoked properly, and abusing him in obscene language if he refused. That was the worst part – he thought he could buy my brain and tongue as well as my body! When he was very naughty and spat out the Martini, I had to take down his shorts and pinch his penis or smack his bottom. After an hour or two I was thoroughly exhausted and fed up, but he was wanking away, and finally fell asleep. I don't think he even came. So I took the money, which he'd put on the table, and ran off, and never went back there again.'

There followed another lull in the conversation, while we refilled our glasses and took platefuls of cherries and strawberries. Madame regarded me quizzically.

'I would guess, Monsieur Smith, that you yourself are somewhat humiliated on behalf of your sex. Would I be right?'

'Oh God, yes!' I exclaimed. 'Though I can't help wondering whether some men don't have gentler, less bizarre fantasies which would be pleasing to women as well.'

'Not in my experience!' chimed in Chantal. 'And if you had heard the women in that brothel talking, you would see what I mean. Worse still, lots of their clients had scatological fantasies, and wanted just to cover women in the vilest mess, even in vomit. And then, worst of all, there was coprophagy!'

'But such men are sick,' I protested. 'They are perverts in the clinical sense, they need treatment. And

94

there are women as well who have that sort of aberration.'

'Not so many,' said Madame ominously.

I felt that these were skirmishes on the edge of a sexual battlefield where I would be bound to be defeated, so I tried another tack.

'Madame Chantal, since you know about sexual fantasy from both viewpoints, won't you please tell me more generally why you find women's imagination so exciting, and men's so repellant and despicable?'

She thought for a moment before replying, and lit a long, slim cigarette, looking for all the world like an effeminate young aesthete of the 1890s trying to be manly. I was unbelievably thrilled by her physical presence and style and wished, hope against hope, that she would ask me to go up to her bedroom that night. Yet that would have contravened the whole ethos of prostitution – what's done is done – and defied the fate of men, to yearn after the perpetually unattainable whore. Then she spoke.

'Perhaps you have noticed here that, however aberrant our fantasies, they always focus on our own bodies, and the body of the man. So-called "normal" sex – fucking and so on – are an integral and central part of our fantasies. You could say that female fantasy consists of embellishing, or ritualising, the sex act. Whereas with men, there is always a strong element of fetishism, which disintegrates that world. Objects are taken out of the sexual context, away from their function, and venerated for their own sake. The phallus is adored or abased (which is only another form of adoration) and something trivial like a woman's stocking or bra is elevated into an object of obsessive desire. Also, as my story shows, men import into their fantasies all the power and trappings which they enjoy (and women don't) in public life. In a brothel such as I described, even nonentities can be celebrities. They become brigadiers or Nazi leaders and force women into the most abject roles to exalt themselves. What I really mean is, they bring social distinctions and their own power in public life into the private, egalitarian world of sex. Women never do. That's why their sexual life is gentler, more anarchic.'

She had spoken with such clarity and persuasiveness that I felt sure that she must have read something about the subject, for her conclusions were too theoretical to be based on a few bizarre experiences.

'Now you will think that I am a feminist, *n'est-ce pas?*" She said this with such a charming smile that I laughed and leant over to touch her hand.

'I like feminists,' I said. 'I'm one myself.'

But Madame evidently decided that I had broken some unwritten and inexorable rule of house etiquette in touching Chantal's hand in public, for she got up abruptly, saying 'And now we must bid you goodnight, Monsieur Smith. Sleep well! Chantal, come to my study for a few minutes. We must discuss the arrangements for the new arrival.'

They departed without a backward glance at me, and I was left disappointed and piqued, especially by Madame's last remark, which I took to refer to the other man who was expected this week. I imagined them making plans for Chantal to re-enact her masked fantasy with the newcomer, and found that the thought gave me acute pain. Ridiculous – or so I told myself as I crossed the moonlit lawn. I lay in bed under a light sheet, so warm was the night. But I was still haunted by visions of the feline girl – or the anthropomorphic cat – and saw my cock stirring under the cover each time she prowled across my imagination.

The Archivist

I woke to the sound of pelting rain, which came as a relief after the increasingly sultry days and made me feel fresh and energetic. It was years since I had felt so healthy – clearly the regime of good food and frequent debauchery suited my constitution, and I had a constant, sensuous awareness of my body. Virginie appeared, again without knocking, as I was having a shower, and stood in the bathroom doorway, leering at me as I soaped myself. She evidently saw such intimacy with the guests as her prerogative. She told me the number of the room where I should go after lunch, and said that storms were forecast. She then volunteered to help me dry myself and, despite my protests, rubbed me all over with the towel, none too gently, then curtseyed to me ironically and tripped away. I was increasingly confused as to whether she was one of the girls available to me, or whether her role was that of the eunuch in the seraglio. Clearly I was available to Virginie, or so she thought.

I tackled the croissants with a hearty appetite and would have liked to go for a walk afterwards, but the rain was too persistent. It was just the morning for the library, however, so I took my notebook and established myself there at the large desk in the window. My head was still full of the events of the day before and the conversation over dinner. But when I tried to make notes on Chantal's story, the masked image of her disturbed me. I speculated that the vileness of her experiences in Cannes had made her into a mask fetishist. After all, the face is as private as the soul – one only wants to reveal it to those one can trust, which is why people wear real and metaphorical masks in their daily life. Perhaps, feeling the awful vulnerability of her face in front of those sadists had decided her never to meet a man again without protection? This line of thought reminded me of that other part of her anatomy that had so fascinated me, and I went to the bookshelves. I found a ten-volume *Universal Encyclopaedia* and took down the volume G-H. Under 'Hermaphrodite' I found an entry running to several columns. It appeared that there was a good deal of learned disputation as to whether the true hermaphrodite existed. Men with fully-formed breasts were common, but there was no medical record of a creature with both penis and vagina. However, travellers' tales often reported such phenomena in faraway places like the Virgin Islands while a number of travelling fairs in the last century claimed to have in their freak-shows hermaphrodites who were 'capable of both sexual roles', as the encyclopaedia delicately put it. A whole section was devoted to 'Bearded Women', which concluded that these, like breasted men, simply suffered from hormonal imbalance. I hoped they saw it that way too. 'Hermaphrodites in Fiction' tickled me, and I discovered that in many fictional utopias or similar imaginary works hermaphrodites were the chosen ideal race because of their reputed power of self-fertilisation – so efficient, compared with our own hit-and-miss methods. Being a modern edition, the entry concluded with an account of the various sex-change operations possible for men. Even surgery is male-dominated, I reflected, since little had apparently been done on sex-changes for women – they had to content themselves with looking butch.

Most intriguing were the engravings and photos of various quasi-hermaphrodites. It showed several fat adolescent boys with tiny cocks, pubescent breasts and womanly hips. The pathos of these photos was immense. No doubt they were accustomed to being examined as medical curiosities, but they stood there abashed, as if they desperately longed to hide their sexual anomalies from the probing camera. Their faces were hauntingly ambiguous, painfully pretty. I imagined vividly the double joy of sex with a hermaphrodite, the simultaneous penetration of every orifice . . . Eventually I made a few sketches and returned the book to its shelf, still frustrated by the mystery of Chantal's appendage, for nothing was said there about the clitoris – although Freud, we know, treats it as a residual penis.

My notebook held various cryptic thoughts which I wanted to elaborate. The film equipment everywhere was easy to explain: women obviously enjoy spectator sex as much as men. But the video playback machinery seemed significant. Do women want to relive their fantasies, whereas men do not? For many men, I thought, the final act of ejaculation was a purge of what had gone before. They are, as it were, emptied and cleaned and forget at once the preliminaries which brought them to orgasm. But the woman ends up *filled*; inside her is a wet, physical reminder of the preceding events, which cannot be forgotten. As soon as I had written this, an alternative explanation formulated itself: perhaps women can replay their fantasies because these are not innately vile or shameful, whereas men in their everyday state of mind would be ashamed to relive the sadistic rites that they had initiated behind locked doors. For myself, I felt nothing but enjoyment and stimulation on viewing the playback of my activities with Julie and Florence, and I longed to see myself and Chantal on the video-screen, but these were their fantasies, not mine. 'Women,' I concluded the page, 'are nearer to the physicality of sex than men, and do not need to repudiate it afterwards. But is this closeness, their earthiness, inherent, or is it conditioned by a social environment which secludes them in house or harem where they have little else to think about or do?'

The answer to this last question, I felt, must lie in anthropologists' studies of women in other cultures, so I looked for books on primitive tribes, of which there were many on the same shelf as Liebknecht and Delamare. They ranged from Diderot's imaginary *Supplément du Voyage de Bougainville*, about free love in an idealised Tahiti, to that modern classic about adolescent girls, *Growing Up In Samoa*. Sandwiched between these were many other books, containing a wealth of information and I spent hours skimming through these. A theory took shape in my mind. Restif de la Bretonne's sexual utopia, *L'Andrographe*, was there, and it was manifest that this libertine had drawn up a sexual penal code which was far harsher to women. For example, marriage was compulsory for women, and any girl who refused an offer was to be given to blind men or cripples as a punishment. When I thought of our own culture until very recently, this severity was also evident, even if promiscuous women usually received not legal but social punishment for their lapses. As I looked at descriptions of tribal behaviour, the pattern was repeated. Although free love may be accepted, women's sexuality is still subject to endless, minute regulation: adolescent girls are segregated, as are women during menstruation. Among some peoples, a woman who has difficulty in labour will be killed along with her child, as painful childbirth signifies the curse of an evil spirit.

As I tried to order all this evidence and reach some conclusion, I found almost the exact formulation that I was searching for in a book by an English anthropologist of the early twentieth century. 'Women,' he wrote 'are superstitiously regarded in primitive tribes as being in direct communion with nature and the physical world. Society is the realm of *men*, but it is constantly threatened by the encroachment of natural forces, which must be mastered at all costs. The ambiguous role of women, part social, part natural, therefore renders them subject to very strong restrictions by men, lest they should become the vehicle whereby Nature invades and destroys the social entity. In some tribes women are sent out into the woods at certain times of the month, to avoid pollution of the village, and so that they can communicate with their governing spirits who dwell in the trees. It is because the woman is the locus of these anarchic or magical forces that she is feared, and must be subdued, and her animal sexuality is usually the starting point for this subjugation.'

I could add nothing to this, but it was tempting to relate it to Chantal's escapades in Cannes. Why had her first client tried to regulate, humiliate and punish her, if not for just such reasons? And why did both men deny *her* sexuality by refusing to touch her, while fetishistically satisfying themselves, if not through fear? Of course, modern man is no savage: he cannot consciously identify woman with the threatening forces of nature, or act upon such a superstition. But civilisation is a thin veneer laid over our previous selves, and once something like the regulation of women's sexuality is turned into laws and conventions, there is no need to refer back to the original reason for the outrage. I meditated that if the myth of Woman as Nature Untamed had a grain of truth, it would explain the special appeal of female fantasy, if men could forget their superstitious fears. Because women's sexual desires are instinctual – unsocialised and unfetishised – they attain a pitch of liberation and ecstasy denied to men.

My conjectures were getting wilder, so I left this point and passed on to what Chantal had said so emphatically about men and money, which reminded me of something I once remembered reading. What was it? And why should the fact that men have the money so completely dominate and pervert their fantasies? The filing system of the mind is a wonderful thing: after a few minutes it threw out the name 'Marx'. I doubted that I would find any of his works in this library, however daring it might be in other respects, but I dug around in what seemed to be the philosophy section and was surprised to find four indexed volumes of his selected works. Then it was only a matter of time before I traced the passage I had vaguely remembered: 'The properties of money are its owner's properties. I am ugly, but I can buy myself the most beautiful of women. Consequently I am not ugly, for the effect of ugliness, its power of repulsion, is annulled by money'. I copied down the quotation, then felt that I had played the archivist for long enough, and left the library, wearied by the unaccustomed intellectual exercise.

Shortly after I got back to my room, the punctual Virginie brought my lunch and I decided to watch the TV as I ate. This time I thought at first that I had turned on the wrong channel, because the picture showed well-dressed people arriving at a cocktail party. I checked, but the set was still tuned to the private channel, so I kept watching. Among the crowd of guests sipping champagne and Manhattans and talking volubly (although the film was once again silent), the camera soon singled out an attractive woman who looked like a surprised, thoroughbred horse, wearing a smart suit and a great deal of costume jewellery. She was talking vivaciously to three or four admirers, one of whom was perhaps her husband, because she turned to him occasionally, as if for confirmation of what she had just said, and laid her hand on his arm. Another man came over to the group and pushed in beside her. He was tall and thickset, with dark hair and a fierce, handsome face, although his tasteful attire belied this savage appearance. He addressed himself to the woman, but she continued to look at the other men, and seemed to ignore him. So he gave his glass to another man in the circle to hold, and put both his hands on her full, high breasts, while she continued talking, taking not the slightest notice.

A waiter came round to refill the glasses and the circle broke up for an instant, then reformed, talking more intensely than before. The savage took the glass from the woman's hand and helped her off with the jacket of her suit as she talked. Then he pushed right into the centre of the circle to stand in front of her, and started to undo her blouse, which fastened by a series of ties. At this juncture, the husband started forward as if to push himself between them, but another guest restrained him, and engaged him in conversation. Meanwhile, the blouse was open to the waist, revealing a low-cut bra over which her generous breasts bulged. The man believed in adversity, for rather than undoing the bra at the back, he tussled with the fastenings of each strap. One was undone, and he pulled down the cup, releasing a shapely breast which fell forward like a luscious, exotic fruit. The woman talked on, oblivious. The other strap soon followed, and the bra fell to her waist. The savage guest stood back to admire his handiwork, and invited the others to do so too. One or two of the men in the group stepped forward and fondled her breasts politely, as if checking them for size and quality, then resumed their conversation.

Then the man crouched down on the ground and put his head inside her pleated skirt, and for some time all that could be seen was the bulge of his head moving in and out. Her panties trickled down her legs and came to rest at her ankles. The waiter came past again, and paused to pour a little champagne over each breast, then went his way. Somebody excused himself and left the

106

circle, but another took his place, shaking hands with everyone as he arrived, and patting each of the woman's breasts. At last the savage emerged, his tie awry and hair ruffled, and he gave the woman's glass to somebody, then took her by the hand and laid her gently on the floor in the middle of the circle, which expanded slightly to make room. He pulled up her skirt over her face: below was a tight, black corset with suspenders. He spread her legs meticulously as far as the corset allowed, then unzipped his flies, pulled out his prick, knelt between her legs and calmly began to fuck her, sometimes taking a sip of his cocktail to refresh himself. The woman lay still. The final shot in the film showed the other men, one by one unzipping their trousers, while continuing their animated conversation. I found that my lunch was cold. I switched off and finished quickly, feeling so randy that I wanted to get to my next assignation as soon as possible.

The Brass Room

I knocked at the door and went straight in, as Virginie
had instructed. This was an old-fashioned bedroom,
with flowered wallpaper and chintz curtains. The only
furniture was a couple of chairs, a dressing table,
cluttered with perfume bottles and make-up, and a
double bed with brass rails. The rain raged outside the
window. Nobody was in the room, but I heard the sound
of a shower running in an adjoining room, to which the
door stood open, so I called out that I had arrived. The
water stopped and a moment later a woman came into
the bedroom, wrapped in a long, navy bathrobe. Her
hair was bright red and long – hennaed, I thought, for
her face had none of the pallor of a natural redhead. She
was perhaps thirty, and had a hard, attractive face with
slanting brown eyes which romantic novelists would
have described as 'smouldering'. Her skin was
suntanned, and the vivid red lipstick which she wore
emphasised her large mouth. The voluminous robe

smothered her figure, but beneath it I saw elegant feet with red-painted toenails.

She did not greet me, but came over to where I stood, put her arms round me, and started to kiss me passionately. As a rule, I do not enjoy kissing whores: it seems such an intimate activity that I reserve it for those I love. Some religions say that a man's soul is in his sperm, but I suspect that mine inhabits my mouth. However, the rules of the house made me comply, and I found myself, despite myself, thrilling to her treatment. A taste of sweet chocolate lingered in her mouth. Her tongue was smooth and lissom, and forced its way round my mouth, licking my own tongue and teeth and seeking out those soft regions where every sensation is magnified a hundred times.

Her approach was very direct: having run her hands cursorily over my back and shoulders, she reached down in front, unerringly chose the right pocket, and put in her hand. She grasped my cock through the thin cotton lining and frigged it as thoroughly as the intervening pocket allowed. Although my imagination was not at all inflamed by this way of proceeding, my nervous system betrayed me, and soon the adrenalin was pumping through my head, and I became very stiff. Following the usual conventions, I slipped my hands inside her robe, and felt around her hips and arse, which were big and firm, with a slightly coarse texture. She was still pleasantly humid from her shower. Keeping the bathrobe discreetly wrapped round her, I insinuated my hands up to her wide, square shoulders, then under her arms to explore her breasts. These were as ample and solid as the rest of her unseen body, and I relished the idea of what is vulgarly called 'getting a handful', and rotated them, alternately, as if I were milking a goat. Meanwhile, she kept kissing me with the same fervour, and her hand in my pocket stimulated me more and more. I dropped her breasts and ran my hands over the tight, convex form of her stomach, delving into the soft hair beneath with a sense of achievement. Sometimes the mind has to take a back seat: sex without embellishments is what the body wants. After watching that perverse film, I was ready for a robust fuck followed by total evacuation of all my pent-up lust. Needless to say, I was disappointed.

Shaking herself free of me, the whore went over to a cupboard set in the wall and invited me to come and look. When she opened it, I thought I was looking at an ironmonger's display window, so full was it of hardware. Heavy brass chains and padlocks, devices that looked like thumbscrews and head-irons, girdles made of brass, and several pairs of manacles, were ranged on the shelves or hanging from hooks at the back. I started laughing, partly out of apprehension, partly because in my various brushes with bondage I had never seen such a comprehensive array. But she looked serious and was reproachful at my levity.

'Are you going to hang me from the ceiling and torture me?' I joked.

'Not at all,' she replied. '*You* are going to chain *me*. But don't forget, my great-grandfather was Houdini.'

I had no idea if this was true, but the challenge excited me. I set about my task with the exaggerated care of the escapist's assistant in a street show, who tries every link in the chain with his own teeth, and invites the strongest man in the audience to test the authenticity of his work. First of all, I carefully disrobed her, and found a strong, tanned, energetic body under the soft towelling, with large breasts well balanced by a big arse. Her pubic hair was, I noticed, brown. With her red hair snaking over the strong shoulders and her open, feral mouth, she looked like an Amazon who only lacked a spear – of which I was glad. I picked up her legs one by one to feel the size of her ankles and calves, then tested each bicep while she held her pose, strangely passive for an Amazon. Since she was the whore here who appealed to me least, I was not sorry that my duty was to manacle her. But as gaoler I was deceptively gentle. I led her over to the bed and placed her on it carefully, face downwards – then, as an afterthought, I turned her face upwards again and ran my fingers lightly over her thighs as if assessing where the first leg-iron would go. When I went to make my selection from the cupboard, I was baffled by the range of choice. A prodigious bunch of keys hung on the door, and I wondered vaguely how, once she was fettered, she could ever be released again since only she knew which key fitted which lock – but this did not worry me unduly. I took over an armful of chains and hand-cuffs at random, and was about to start when she said warningly, 'You can chain me but not touch me.'

This was a different game! I had planned to chain her in a fashion that made her disposable to my needs, but now I resolved to bandage her up like a broken arm. I manacled her ankles together, and wrapped a chain round her knees. Rolling her over brusquely, I locked her hands together behind her back then, for good measure, I wrapped a long chain round her arms and torso, arranging it artistically so as to leave her breasts bare, then cross-winding it to force them closer together and make them bulge like well-upholstered cushions. As a final touch of genius, I added a chain running from her

112

hands, through her legs and up to join the one which pinioned her arms – an impromptu chastity belt, as I informed her. I then sat on the edge of the bed and comtemplated my handiwork. Her eyes had shut and she was breathing heavily: I was not sure whether the prohibition against touching was meant to frustrate her desires or mine. Hers, I concluded, since I felt no special desire to touch her. I rather favoured looking at a girl made into a package.

But the cat-and-mouse instinct lurks somewhere in us all, and after I had watched her for five minutes or so (and noticed her looking at me from between her lashes), and had mentally composed an entry for my diary on this event, which seemed to be something of a cliché as these things go, I decided to do something to her. Touching was forbidden, I reflected, but not indirect contact. I looked round for an intermediary. The first thing I spotted was a silk scarf hung over the back of a chair. With this, I tickled her thoroughly from head to toe, holding it high above her, and letting its feathery tip trail slowly over her exposed breasts. Her skin, though coarse, was very sensitive, and she shivered deeply as the scarf made its way down her body. When I was weary of this occupation, I went to find something else to play with and saw in the hearth an old pair of bellows, which promised to be good fun.

Inflating these, I sent short, cold blasts on to the most tender parts of her unresisting body. Her eyes had been shut, but they opened wide with shock when I blew, first on her nipples, then under her chin. She called me every name under the sun and ordered me to stop, but I was much too amused by my game. I manoeuvred the nozzle of the bellows under her chastity belt and sent a long cold draught into her cunt, then several more, which made her writhe on the bed in rage, and then an even longer, colder one up her arse. 'All good, clean fun,' I thought to myself as I restored the bellows to the fireplace, adding 'She did ask for it!' My inventiveness in evading her taboo now knew no bounds, and I went to the bathroom and filled a glass with warm water, which I slowly poured from a great height over her stomach and pubis while she muttered angrily, 'You wait! I'll piss on you, you bastard!' But then, changing her tone to a cajoling one, she said, 'Now, *chéri*, if you will undo the chains a little, I would like to touch and be touched.'

'But you're very nice as you are, *chérie*,' I returned. 'Nice and helpless.'

But I took that as the lifting of her interdiction and I rolled up my sleeves sat astride her legs, and began to stimulate her breasts and stomach, now one, now the other, by resting my hands on the curving flesh and rocking them heavily to and fro – a movement which seems to awake the nerves embedded deep under the skin and produce a deeper, hungrier arousal than surface sensation. It certainly whetted her appetite, and she begged me to take off her chastity belt and 'get in there', but I went on with my relentless, provoking pressure. When I judged her to be really frantic – although the only way she could show this was by her distraught expression and jerking movements of her body – I stood up and began to undress carefully, while she painfully turned her head to watch greedily. After that I masturbated a little, sitting on the bed beside her face, until my cock looked very threatening. Then at last, I took the bunch of keys to release her – and then was thwarted because I did not know how. She heard my fumblings and explained that each key had a spot of colour which corresponded to that on the padlock. Following this advice, I removed the chain between her legs, and undid her knees and ankles, but immediately fixed each ankle to a bedpost so that she was spread wide, wide open. I unchained her arms and breasts, and attached each wrist to the rail at the head of the bed. Now she was the shape of a perfect St Andrew's cross. So that she should not feel too liberated, I wrapped a chain loosely round her throat several times, and locked that to the bedhead too. As a finishing touch, I took one of the brass girdles and encircled her waist with it tightly: it served no purpose but make her look the slave more completely.

'You're very conscientious,' she groaned, as she found herself trussed up like one of the ring-necked African women, and unable to lift her head.

'Since you can't see what's going on,' I said to her magnanimously, 'I'll tell you what I am going to do. First of all, I shall rub my prick, which is large as a prize marrow, over your pneumatic breasts, and then beat it on your belly, whose skin is stretched tight as a drum.'

I ran out of literary style at that point, so I rubbed myself all over her, delighting in her captivity. She responded noisily, and bluntly told me to 'get on with it, for Heaven's sake'. Feeling contrary, I redoubled my attention to the rest of her body, avoiding any contact with her hungry cunt, and instead pinching her nipples, armpits, nose, anything that came to hand. But by now she was extremely angry, and though she might have been play-acting I remembered my obligation to be obedient.

'Now,' I announced 'My great Zeppelin is going to fly

into your rainy cunt.' (I had long ago found that flowery, obscene language, embarrassing as it is to invent, has a very rewarding effect, even on hardened whores.)

This news alerted her body, which stiffened and seemed to burn with desire for this act of consummation that it had so long anticipated and been denied. The entrance was wide open and wet between her splayed-out legs, and although my cock had reached its full size or more, it glided in, like a submarine rather than a Zeppelin, into the subaqueous world of her cunt. Excited though I was by this time, I felt at my ease because my helpless partner was unable to make any demands on me, nor could she, by an untimely movement, destroy the rhythm which I set up to please myself best. I had never considered the advantages of necrophilia before, but now I could see the attraction. I screwed her in a leisurely way, sometimes resting on top of her, squashing her big breasts outwards, sometimes balancing on my hands and feet, with arched body, so that she should feel nothing of me except that focal point of pleasure.

I perfected a trick which drove her to distraction, withdrawing from her long enough for her to think I had stopped entirely, then going in again at the speed of a snail. But, though I was a cunt-teaser, I bore her no ill-will, so that when she asked me desperately to 'finish me off' I went in with mighty strokes, which made her shudder and contort her limbs as though she would break her fetters, and I felt the lips of her cunt swelling and gripping me tighter even as it ran with moisture. When I saw that she was coming, I twisted and pushed in like a savage engine. I felt the orgasm shake her whole body, but she made no sound – perhaps Amazons don't.

Afterwards, she mildly asked me to undo her legs because they hurt, and when I released all her chains, she rolled over on her side, head cushioned on her arm, and fell asleep. But I felt that I had not yet received my dismissal so I stretched out on the bed beside her and toyed with myself a little. I noticed a book on the floor beside the bed and picked it up. Surprisingly, it was a book of readings from contemporary French philosophers, with headings such as 'Nothingness and Being' and 'The Self and the Other'. What could a girl like this want with a book like that? I started to read about the permanent tension between Self and Other, which seemed to relate to sexual fantasy as well as anything, when a voice close to me said 'It's your turn now.' She was awake again.

'So you're a philosopher, are you?' I asked.

'What?' She sounded defensive. 'Oh, that book. It's not mine, I just found it there,' she added vaguely. Then she got up and told me to come and sit in a chair. Perhaps sex fuddles the brain – I did not guess what was going to happen until I heard something jangling behind me. The chair was very upright, with a runged wooden back, and she drew my arms through the gaps and handcuffed them there, so securely that my upper half was entirely unable to move. A chain was quickly passed round my waist from behind, pinning my back flat to that of the chair and forcing me into a more rigorous posture than I am accustomed to. She fastened each ankle to a chair leg, and my immobility was total. But her fantasy was not, it seemed, for she brought out of the cupboard a little cage made of brass strips, long and round, which she slipped over my cock. It fitted well for length, but I found the diameter constricting, although the constant pressure was not unwelcome. The last addition to the decor was the silk scarf, with which she gagged me soundly – to stop me screaming, I imagined, and steeled myself for some act of cruelty.

Video recordings I knew by now, but this girl seemed to want a live replay of the previous events, with roles reversed. She ran her hands temptingly over my body, then poked my cock in its tight muzzle with her fingers, waking the slumbering beast. An infinite progression set in: the bigger it got, the tighter the cage, the greater the pressure, the bigger it got – and so on. In such a context you forget to distinguish between pain and pleasure in any case. But now she knelt in front of me and began to masturbate, and the charm of the sight made me hungry for her as I had not been earlier. I could not move an inch, let alone touch her, and my body felt like one enormous itch, which longed for her soothing hand – but her hands were busily working between her legs. She looked at me mockingly and asked me what I would like her to do to me, a question which put my mind in a spin but which as she well knew, my mouth could not answer. Then she moved an easy chair to face me and sprawled in it, her legs apart, so that I saw right into her cunt. She inserted two fingers and slid them in and out, imitating my bawdy patter. 'Now I am putting the giant cucumber of my finger between my legs,' and so on. On my prison chair, I felt abandoned and sick with desire, and rolled my eyes wildly, appealing to her to free, or at least to touch me. But she had business of her own, and I had to wait until she had come again, and lay back in the chair, lips parted in a smile of deep self-satisfaction.

At length she took pity on me and came over and started massaging my nipples, which were hard and

118

insufferably sensitive. Could I come inside the brass cage? I wondered, and, looking down, saw that it had a convenient hole in the brass cap at the end. Again, she probed and compressed my prick through the holes between the bars, send shocks of pleasure along my spine. My impotence in every other limb and organ made this one all the more profligate. Sensing this, she seized my balls, and with a crescendo of skilful, rapid movements, which set my blood dancing, she made me come – before I was ready, against my will, yet all the better for that. My spunk shot through the brass hole with great force and covered her breasts, but she only laughed.

She went off to the bathroom and was there so long without making a noise that I feared she had left by another door and was abandoning me like this as part of some arcane code of punishment. In my state of helplessness and satiation I could do nothing but await her return, and eventually she reappeared and put on her robe again. Then she freed me, and helped rub my cramped limbs that still bore the imprint of the chains, as my cock did of its bars. She offered me a bath, but I said I preferred to wash in the privacy of my own room. She was amused – I had forgotten that my rooms were probably the least private of any in the house. She watched silently as I dressed, and came and gave me a kiss on the cheek as I was leaving – then called me back. When I turned, she held out the brass cage to me.

'Here, take this,' she said. 'It was made in France. It can be your souvenir!'

Paradise Invaded

Virginie had an uncanny instinct for divining when I was in bed and, as I dozed fitfully after my escape, she knocked loudly enough to wake me and came in. Familiarly, she sat on the edge of the bed and said 'I have a message for you from Madame. Could you come over at seven tonight, as the new guest has arrived?' I answered sleepily, 'With pleasure – what time is it now?'

'Quarter to seven,' she said triumphantly, and vanished in a flurry of apron and legs. I dragged myself out of bed for a quick shower and put on the better of my two suits, with the childish intention of impressing the newcomer. At the very mention of his arrival I felt threatened: paradise was invaded and Adam had a rival for Eve's attentions. On the other hand, the thought of a little male company was agreeable, if only for the sake of contrast, since I had not even heard a male voice since my conversation with the village odd-job man, days ago – and that had hardly been scintillating. I added a flashy striped tie, of which Madame would surely disapprove and, my dress complete, sauntered across to the house, asserting my territorial rights by cutting across the lawn and going in through the French windows, like an *habitué*.

My hostess was in an easy chair, reading the *Illustrated London News* – or at least, as I saw when she put it down, looking at the photos beside the gossip column. She greeted me with unusual warmth: perhaps she was perceptive enough to see that I felt ill-at-ease over the new arrival. She even complimented me on my tie! Then she asked me to sit down and pressed a large whisky into my hand.

'I wanted to have a word with you, Monsieur Smith, before Monsieur Lalande comes over, to explain the arrangements. His suite is in the converted barn, so you will not be troubled by any noise, or comings and goings. Like you, he will take most of his meals in his room unless, of course, you prefer to eat together. In the evening we can all dine here, which will be amusing. Is that satisfactory?'

Of course, I said. But there was one question I was dying to ask, though I found no way to phrase it delicately.

'Does he – will he – er – Will he be seeing the same women that I have seen?' I was thinking of Chantal, though I had no earthly right to think proprietorially of anyone in this place.

'Probably not,' said Madame, appreciating that I needed reassurance. 'As you may have realised, my colleagues here come and go as they please, a few days now and then, and I have a constantly changing group in the house.'

I was amused to hear the whores being elevated to 'colleagues'. Her frank answer emboldened me to ask a question that had gnawed me like vermin for days. 'Can I ask you how you select the – colleagues – which each client sees?'

'Certainly. When someone arrives all of us who are in the house have a look at him on the closed-circuit system, and those who like the look of him tell me. Also, I have a good idea of the kind of men who interest each of my colleagues, so that I ring them up in Paris if someone particularly suitable comes, and they arrange a visit.'

This pleased me because I thought that the golden-haired arrival of the previous day must have been summoned because of her special compatibility with me. Yet I had seen no sign of her. Perhaps she had been called to meet Monsieur Lalande? I ventured another question.

'Doesn't it happen sometimes that a man arrives who nobody fancies? What happens then?'

'That is very rare because my contacts in Paris such as Madame Mirabelle carry out a thorough suitability test before recommending someone. But it sometimes happens that a man comes who appeals to nobody: then, rather than disappoint him, we draw lots. But not many women can enact fantasies with someone who displeases them unless, for example, the fantasy is rape.'

This explanation threw a new, less flattering light on my encounter with Madame Mirabelle; had it only been in the course of duty that she opened her legs to me so freely? Everything I learnt in this puzzling household cast doubt on some previous certainty, as sodium lighting changes the colour of everyday things in the

123

street. But now someone approached down the corridor and we both stood up to greet the new guest. Monsieur Lalande was a tall, handsome fellow, a few years older than myself, I guessed. He was ebony black and his features looked Ethiopian to me, but he spoke French like a native and, when we fell into English, he spoke it with an Oxford accent. Both his manners and his three-piece cream suit exuded the confidence which only wealth brings. On being introduced, he grasped my hand tightly and said 'How do you do, Monsieur Smith? I've heard so much about you!' That remark always makes my tongue cleave drily to the roof of my mouth, but in this context I was even more horrified. But I later thought that maybe Virginie had prattled about me as she showed him my room, or even that it was an empty formula of *politesse*.

We sat down to have an aperitif before dinner, and it became clear that Madame and Lalande were old friends, from their shared acquaintances and the tenor of their conversation. He showed the utmost courtesy towards me, trying to draw me into the talk by asking questions, and saying that he had been educated for a few years in England, and did I know? . . . and had I seen? . . . and so on. I explained that I had been out of the country for many years and was not at all *au fait* with London social life, a rather imprudent response, since it lopped off a promising branch of conversation. But by the time Virginie brought in a steaming pot of onion soup, I was more relaxed, though not exactly at ease. Madame and Lalande talked constantly, which at least concealed my silence. What distressed me about the situation most was the loss of the intimate dinnertime conversations with Madame – partly because I thought we could never discuss sex so freely in front of a third person, partly because, as I now realised, I was flattered by this lady's exclusive attention even if she was, in the final analysis, no more than a pimp.

When I thought it would be downright rude to remain silent any longer, I gauchely asked Monsieur Lalande 'Do you come here often, Monsieur?'

'As often as I can make it, Monsieur. Usually once every two or three weeks.'

What extravagant debauchery! I was astounded. Then he added, 'But usually only for one night. Fortunately, this time I can stay until Wednesday morning, because I am on my way to see someone in Marseilles. Madame de Rochevillier looks very healthy for her age, but I still like to keep an eye on her.'

There were too many gaps in this cryptic puzzle for me to understand.

'But I thought everyone stayed here for at least a week?' I said pleadingly to Madame.

'Yes, indeed, our clients do,' she laughed. 'But this is my physician.'

I laughed too, with relief that must have been evident to them both. All sorts of pieces slipped into place in the puzzle: the 'new arrival' must have been the woman who came yesterday, rather than Dr Lalande. His enviable familiarity and ease with Madame were also explained. All the same, I thought she had played me a mean trick, as she had unquestionably misled me to think that the new 'guest' was another customer who had come for some time. Instinct told me that this deception had been part of a carefully laid plan – devilish feminists at work again! – to prevent my becoming over-confident, or complacent about my role of reigning pasha. My sense of relief was almost instantly overturned by Monsieur Lalande, who said, winking at me, 'Although I came to see Madame, I'm not unwilling to visit the other inhabitants of the house if required.'

I was left entirely unsure as to whether this was a man-to-man comment, as the wink suggested, or a physician's remark, and the wink merely an aberration. I spent the rest of the meal observing Lalande's left eye for any sign of a tic, but I saw none. His appetite was in proportion to his height, which must have been well over six foot, mine was sharpened by the ordeal of that afternoon, and age had certainly not blunted Madame's. We ate our way through thick veal cutlets, a huge plate of cheeses and a delectable *tarte tatin*, and then settled down to coffee and brandy. Monsieur Lalande then addressed me again, this time in meticulous English.

'Madame has told me of your fascinating work on female sexuality, Monsieur. I wonder if you would permit me to offer you a little anecdote that came my way in the course of my professional duties?' Nothing would please me more, said I.

'It happened in the South of France to a daughter of one of my patients, who mostly lived round there. She was a pretty, innocent girl of sixteen and was out walking in the hills near her village one day, when a young man – the son of a local smallholder, it turned out – appeared from behind the olive trees and tried to kiss her. She was frightened and tried to run away, so he grabbed her, threw her to the ground and well and truly raped her – so drastically, in fact that she had to be sewn up again at the local hospital. Afterwards, the young man was aghast at what he had done – what started out as a bit of pastoral ribaldry nearly ended in her death. He visited her in hospital, then gave himself up to the police. With a lenient judge and a good character, he got off with only a year in prison. The day he came out, he went round to the girl's house and proposed to her. And it ended like all good fairy stories: they got married and lived happily ever after, and now he can rape her every night of the year. What do you make of that, Monsieur Smith? Surely this proves that women share men's fantasy of violence? In my view, all women are willing victims, masochists at heart.'

I mumbled something about one swallow not making a summer. In truth, my reaction to the disturbing story was so mixed that I wanted to think about it, and could not oblige him with the easy agreement that he demanded.

'And I could give you another example, about my own country, where in some parts we still have the barbaric custom of infibulation. On the wedding night . . .'

'Excuse me, I must go, I'm very tired this evening,' I interrupted precipitously, feeling sick as I guessed how the next story would end. Charming company though he was, I could see the doctor's anecdotes prolonging themselves into a direful *Decameron* where the link between them was not buckets of shit poured on to innocent heads, but the rupture of women's flesh and sinews, and the outpouring of their blood. He was surprised to be cut short, but both he and Madame got up and shook hands with me, then sat down again to continue their gossip about Parisian high society.

Wet Dreams

Back in my room, I tried to expel Dr Lalande and his gory histories from my mind by reading a book which I had borrowed from the library about the female orgasm, from which I hoped to glean some hints about the distinctive needs of the opposite sex and which might lead me to a better understanding of women's fantasy life. Outside, the predicted thunderstorm had at last arrived, and my room was made lurid by violent flashes. I drew the curtains and began to savour that familiar pleasure of my student days – putting up my feet in a warm room to read a good book. I was immersed in the most complicated diagrams of the female reproductive organs – the author believed in starting with basics – when I thought I heard someone at the door. Reverberating thunder made it impossible to be sure, but I listened and again thought I heard a tap. I went and flung open the door, and found a drenched girl outside. I brought her into the room and made her sit down. She wore a full, dark cape, which was soaking wet, and high, black boots which disappeared up under the long cape. Her hair was dark and would have been curly had it not been plastered to her head in straggling strands. But her narrow, heart-shaped face seemed untouched by the rain: I saw sad, dark eyes, a fine nose, and a wide, sculptured mouth. She was younger than the other women here.

'Would you like a towel for your hair?'

She declined.

'What can I do for you, Mademoiselle?'

'I was going to ask you to my room tonight, but with this marvellous storm I thought the garden would be better.' Her voice was young and buoyant; she spoke with the enthusiasm of a lover making a date, not like a courtesan to a customer.

'Isn't the garden rather wet – and dangerous, with so much lightning?' I heard myself sounding old and stuffy.

'But it's so *lovely* in the rain – and lightning is so *thrilling*!'

I resigned myself to the most uncomfortable fantasy yet, and picked up my umbrella.

'No, you won't be needing *that*.' When she laughed, she was impish, spellbinding. 'And you must take off your suit, or it will spoil.'

So I did, stopping at my shirt and pants to ask 'Is this all right?'

'You'll only get them soaked. Do take everything off.'

'But I can't go out undressed like that,' I protested. 'What about Madame and Lalande?'

'Don't worry, they've been in bed for *ages*.' I noted the ambiguity of this remark.

When I was naked, she smiled as if pleased by the

sight, and led me out of the garden into the storm. The first thing I noticed was how warm and pleasant the rain was. The heart of the storm had receded and the lightning only lit up the garden sporadically. We went towards the cluster of trees at my end of the lawn, and stopped. Her cape had arm-slits, which I had not observed before, and now she put her hands out through them and touched my body under the arms, running her hands down over the ribs, round the prominence of the hips, and down my thighs. My body was wet, but not at all cold, and her hands ran over it, exploring every inch tenderly. I reached out to find the opening of her cape, which was buttoned. I undid two large buttons and put my hands inside. Underneath she was dry, warm and naked. My hands slid over a body so smooth it seemed polished. I could feel large bones inside a slim body: cascading breasts with large, puckered nipples, a barely rounded stomach which breathed faster as I discovered it. But now I wanted her to be equal with me in my nakedness, so I undid the rest of the buttons and tossed away the cape.

As the rain washed over her body, making it shine, I rejoiced in the sight, for she was a true sylph, thin, fragile, yet voluptuous: her boots reached halfway up her thighs, turning her into a creature of fantasy. In the meagre light reflected from the semi-luminous sky, I could faintly see the triangle of hair at the top of her legs. Then a lightning flash and suddenly eyes, nipples and maiden hair stood out vividly for an instant, alluring landmarks in a sea of milky flesh. I was too overcome to know what to do next; I told her she was beautiful, then surrounded her fairy body with my arms and pressed it to me, her wetness against mine. Wet skin against wet skin

131

is supremely erotic – we both felt the magnetism, but she slipped from me like an eel and ran across the lawn with such gracefulness that I pursued her, wanting to capture it for myself. Then she doubled back, eluding me again, and ran into the trees, where began a dreamlike game of hide-and-seek.

Flashes of white glistening flesh showed here and there – in a bush, behind the trunk of a beech – and I followed as she darted away. When I lost sight of her altogether, I would hear a low whistle from a new direction and follow it. The rain beat down, covering me with a warm outer skin, but somehow the moon appeared between the flying clouds and there was my wood-nymph, standing straight and watchful beside a silver birch. This time I caught her and began to caress her insubstantial, watery body, and this time she submitted to my touch.

She led me beneath the hanging willow, where the grass was almost dry, and we began to make love in earnest, our bodies fraught with desire. Her hands wandered all over me, transmitting young life and energy. I pushed her up against the bole of the tree and pressed myself on to her urgently, then kissed her wet face here and there – eyes, nose, cheeks – and finally fastened myself to her mouth, sucking, biting her lips, snaking my tongue in between them to meet hers. Then I bent down, nuzzling at the damp patch of hair, nibbling the skin beneath it, more like a puppy-dog than a man. Her piquant, fishy flavour sharpened my appetite, and she moved her legs apart so that I could feed to my heart's content, while she tousled my wet hair above. I had a burning desire to be inside her now, and stood up in front of her as she leant back against the rough trunk, and with one hand I felt blindly between her legs to make my entrance. The lips of her cunt were gorged with blood and parted willingly to welcome my exigent cock, which was soon in her warm, slanting passage. Perhaps because she was so young, the mouth of her vagina was deliciously tight, and its walls so elastic that they gripped me incessantly bringing me almost to the point of climax every time I moved inside.

'Ah, so nice, so big,' she murmured, and I felt myself growing even greater.

Standing like that, my every movement produced a relentless friction against her clitoris and soon she was moaning constantly with gratification and clasping my shoulders in an animal need to be closer to me. Her breasts pressed against mine – damp, bulbous flesh with sharpened nipples, which sent thrills through the straining muscles of my chest.

'Let's lie down,' I said at last, dying to feel the full length of my prick sink into her, to reach her soft womb, a luxury which was impossible while we stood like that. She felt the same need, but she took me out from the shelter of the willow into the rain, her natural element, and lay face down on the sodden, earth-scented grass – the nymph supplicating her Mother. Her body was silvered by the transient moon. Again I wondered at its deceptive contours – how could such a voluptuous arse be joined to such slim limbs? Bending over her, I pulled up her haunches and drove into her from behind; this time I was able to bury myself to the very root of my prick, and feel her cunt yield to the ardent invader. At first, I stayed there without moving, so sweet was the sensation of being held tight in that dark cavern. Then I fucked her like a dog, mounting her, pawing her back as

133

I panted, and pushed myself into that sheathlike cunt, and dragged myself out again. Each time I went in, I felt as if my cock had been eaten by a hungry maw. The laboriousness added to my growing excitement, and hers – each movement was so much longer and heavier than when a cunt is wide and wet. I could not see her face and expression, but I heard her call out in delight as I went in ever deeper. At last, I could hold back no longer, and I said, 'I shall explode! Come with me.' The words acted like a trigger, and she came like a wild thing. In that tight enclosure I could feel every spasm that shook her, and she squeezed my come out of me with overwhelming force, as I let myself go and cried out to the moon.

Even then, satiated beyond my dreams, I was reluctant to stop. We held each other and rolled over and over on the grass, forgetful of wetness and mud, mindful only of the other's body, which still tingled with the dying sensation that rippled through the nerve-ends for long afterwards. As the wet earth covered our skins, the rain seemed to wash us clean. Yet when I finally got up to look for her cape I saw before me no nymph but a young savage, face and body streaked with the inexplicable daubings of some esoteric initiation. I told her to come back with me, and to my great surprise, she followed me obediently to my room. There I put on soft lights and ran the bath, while she stood in a corner, vainly trying not to drip on the carpet. I took off her boots, and put her into the bath, then soaped her like a baby with the great, peachy ball of soap, and rubbed my hands over her slippery curving flesh, until I felt desire awaken again. She smiled with content and lay back in the bath, and said I should get in too, since I looked like a chimney-sweep. She washed me in my turn, paying special attention to my tender stirring cock, and giving it the most exquisite massage I had ever experienced with the aid of the lathering soap.

Tired as we both were, our eyes met and agreed that we must fuck again. The rain had only been a prelude to this wettest of fantasies. Her legs were round my hips, my legs stretched out under her, and she sat down over my cock, which floated like some fishy predator, and guided it into that delectable hole once more. Perhaps fucking in space would be like doing it under water? Weightless and frictionless, I floated in and out of her. As the water reduced all sensation, it took longer to reach that plateau of arousal where the next movement seems sure to send you dizzily over the edge – but the journey was blissful! I reached forward to pet her young breasts, still slimy with soap, and slipping from my hands as I tried to surround them and imprison their perfect roundness. She moved over me like an angel fish – hovering, darting this way and that in the stillness of our secret aquarium. And when, grasping the sides of the bath, she swung back and forth, a floating vacuum which drew me along in its wake, faster and faster, I abandoned myself to her utterly, and came as she swallowed me up in her cunt, making the water still wetter.

We took it in turns to towel each other; as her hair began to dry and fall over her face in a tangle of black curls, I saw how pretty she was, and how painfully young. I asked her age and she said, with no show of secrecy, that she was twenty. Some fatherly instinct in me reached out towards her and I said, 'But is this really what you want to do with your life? You're so young, so attractive, you could have a decent job, a nice husband.'

135

'Ah, but you don't understand at all why I'm here,' she said, speaking as if to a backward child, and would say no more. Being close to her body for such a long time had made me feel so attached that parting would be a physical wrench, and I asked her to sleep with me, not knowing whether the rules allowed this, or even whether she would want to. Again she agreed gaily, as if she had already planned this next episode of her elaborate fantasy. But exhaustion had overtaken us both, and we just lay silently with our arms round each other until we slept. I had the sweetest dreams yet, of girls that were trees, and silver birches that were girls, whose lithe, scented trunks I embraced and kissed with loving passion and penetrated with supernatural strength. When I woke in the morning she had slipped away, but I saw her imprint on the pillow and still smelt her hair there, like damp leaves.

Charades

That day there was a variation in what had begun to seem like a regular routine of studious mornings and lecherous afternoons. Virginie told me that I should go to Room 9 immediately after breakfast, where I would find Chloe. As a rule, my libido is not at its strongest at nine-thirty in the morning, but the image of myself as a sexual slave, summoned at Chloe's whim, pleased me immensely, and I began to preen myself, shaving closely the stubble which grows so prolifically when I am sexually active. An accompanying catechism ran through my head. Was it sheer masochism, to enjoy being a sex object for these women, at their beck and call? Surely not, came the reply, because you are equally eager to dominate *them*, and treat them as objects for your lust, when the occasion arises. Is the woman a sadist, who uses a man just to fulfil her sexual needs? Answer: no more than you are a masochist for enjoying it. I had drawn the lesson from the last few days that the greatest delight is to be had in such a way that one uses and is used, turn and turn about. The labels 'sadist' and 'masochist' which had troubled me in the past I would henceforth reserve for the man or woman who becomes stuck in one groove and no longer takes part in the interplay of forces, the ever-changing balance of power. I stopped to take a note of this piece of wisdom before making my way across to Chloe.

Room 9 was on the first floor again, right at the end of the corridor. When I knocked, a musical voice answered '*Entrez*'. The first impression I had was of entering a chaotic theatrical wardrobe, for bright dresses and gaudy costumes hung from pegs on the walls of the room and a tall, old-fashioned hat stand dripped with scarves, necklaces of sparkling stones, glittering belts and feather boas. In the midst of all this stood Chloe, soberly dressed – in the clothes of a billiard-room shark. A black velvet smoking jacket, double-breasted, hung open to show a low-cut waistcoat in figured grey satin, over a ruffled shirt. Tapering black trousers, with a silk stripe each side, ran down to highly polished spats. She even wore a large, black bow tie, inside the open neck of the shirt. This garb was so unexpected in a house where all the women dressed like women – that is to say, in dresses – or like whores – in nothing at all – that I was taken aback. As for the girl inside the costume, Chloe was tall and slight, though her breasts swelled pleasingly under the tight waistcoat. Otherwise, the unfitting bagginess of the men's clothes she wore hid her essential shape. Her face was straight off the cover of *Vogue* – indeed, I was sure I had seen a model who was her double in some magazine – with high cheekbones and hard, perfect features, enhanced by expertly used make-up. Such faces are

138

ageless and timeless. Her brown, straight hair was done in the severest style, parted down the centre and drawn back flat to her head, into a knot at the back, a style which exaggerated her mannish appearance and in no way detracted from her looks. I suspected that she had struck a pose for my arrival, but now she smiled and stepped forward to shake my hand. She spoke very good English, tinged with an American accent.

'I'm so sorry to call you over at this ungodly hour, but I have an engagement in town later today, and I did want to meet you before I left.'

I said I was flattered. She went over to a hi-fi on the floor in a corner, and I looked round the room again. It was luxuriously decorated with paper of some pre-Raphaelite design, but little of this could be seen beneath the clusters of theatrical clothes which smothered the walls. There was a jumble of suitcases, clothes and books spilling out of them, and a writing desk in front of the wide window, covered with letters. Studio cushions abounded, striped in rich, shining materials, and the inevitable television set stood on the floor, half-concealed by a fur coat carelessly flung over it. There was no sign of a bed but several doors led off the room, so presumably Chloe had a suite. As the music started, I heard again the haunting jazz which had drifted across the lawn one evening – its notes held the quintessence of New Orleans of the 1920s. Chloe made me sit down on a cushion and sat facing me, asking me about my travels, my impressions of the United States (where I was sure she had perfected her English) and my research.

'I won't ask you what your conclusions are, Monsieur Smith, as I'm sure we shall see them in print very soon, but I have been following your progress on the small screen with great interest.'

'Oh yes?' I said casually, hoping she would make some favourable comment. I had at last ceased to be embarrassed by this sort of overture, and was greedy for praise – the metamorphosis which takes place at the birth of a star!

'I have seen you play the man so often now, that I would like to observe you in the woman's role.'

At first I did not understand what she meant. But she went over to the wall and took down a long two-piece evening suit in deep gold satin. The skirt was slit audaciously to the thigh; the jacket had a wrap-over front with an extravagantly long tie.

'I think this will fit you nicely. Here, these are for you as well.'

She gave me an assorted handful of shoes, stockings and suspenders, then led the way through one of the doors into the bathroom.

'You can change here,' she said, closing the door. Strange to say, in the length and breadth of my sexual odyssey I had never come across transvestism before but, like most men I suspect, I had deep inside a sneaking longing to see myself in female dress. In my case, this instinct was reinforced by the intellectual conviction that by dressing and acting the woman I might gain an insight into the subject of my research. However, my innocence in these matters meant that I spent a very long time dressing. I was almost defeated by the suspender belt, and as I fought with the snaky monster, the camera in the wall caught my eye and I found myself blushing deeply. At last I was arrayed, and saw a new, elegant self regarding me in the mirror.

Something was missing – my face was wrong. Chloe had thoughtfully left all her cosmetics on the shelf, and I spent a few more minutes with her huge range of lipsticks, eye pencils and mascara, transforming myself into a drag queen. With maroon lipstick and black lines lavished round my eyes, I thought myself a good-looking woman, and added a touch of perfume to complete the illusion. Nothing could be done about my hair, so I combed it fiercely back behind my ears in imitation of Chloe's severe style, and went shyly back for her inspection.

'You look terrific,' was her response. 'Have a whisky.' From somewhere she had procured a tray with glasses, ice and a full bottle of Bourbon. I thought ten o'clock was a little early for such indulgence, but I did not want to spoil her show and I like Bourbon, so I accepted. I was incessantly aware of my borrowed clothes and various discomforts – the precarious swaying of my high-heeled shoes, the irritating tug of the suspenders at the black stockings which they held up, and the cumbersome feeling of the skirt flapping at my ankles. I wondered how women could bear to dress so – so many actions are ruled out that they must feel the prisoners of their clothes. Chloe now changed the record and put on some big-band dance music.

'Shall we dance?' she said.

'I thought you'd never ask.'

We tried to waltz round the room then to tango, but the studio cushions and general disorder made it an imperfect dance-floor. I soon realised that dancing had merely been her excuse to bring us into physical contact – as it so often is in real life – for Chloe's hands skated over the shiny surface of my costume, then lingered on the curve of my buttocks. So this was what it was like to be a woman, a constant prey to the promiscuous depredations of male hands, usually in situations such as dancing, where politeness made protest inappropriate. My tall shoes made me much taller than my partner, so that I looked down on her swept-back hair and could smell the fruity perfume on her neck and shoulders. Satin must be a good conductor for sexual impulses, because the effect of her hand on my arse through the skirt's texture was electrifying. Clad like this, I felt infinitely more sensual than in my own clothes and simultaneously less protected, more assailable. Perhaps the two feelings were not unconnected. Equally poignant was Chloe's transformation into a man: stiff layers of tobacco-scented clothing interposed between her and me. How complete our role reversal was, and whether I was meant to be entirely passive, I did not know, but I keenly wanted to touch her and to equalise the situation where she could reach my most private regions through the thin satin while I could not even feel the outline of her body.

As we swayed half-heartedly in time to the nostalgic music and she continued her sexist spoliation of my body, I reached inside her velvet jacket and clasped her waist, which was more slender than I had guessed. Then, since that was allowed, I undid the shapely waistcoat and ran my hands over her breasts. So fine was the stuff of her shirt that it was as if I touched her skin directly. As I found with my own skintight costume, the mediating material made the sensation even more tantalising, and I wanted to postpone the moment when I would touch her bare tits. This delaying action of our clothes is undoubtedly the definitive argument against nudist camps, I thought, as I fondled her and felt her nipples rise, then fade, then become hard as knots under the pitiless squeezing of my fingers.

Meanwhile, Chloe was tracing the bold slit in my skirt from knee to thigh, then she put her hand through it at the top to enter the world of feminine underwear beneath. She had neglected – deliberately, I did not doubt – to give me any panties, so between the lace of the suspender belt and the fine mesh of my stocking-tops was an indefensible gap where her fingers played on my buttocks, poking into the crevice between their tight cheeks and teasing the sealed secret of my arsehole. I heard her laugh infectiously and looked down; she pointed to where the satin of my skirt billowed out over a prodigious erection.

'Lucky that women don't have one,' she said, and went on teasing with her fingers, while I pressed my living monster in its satin shroud against her until I felt the pressure of her stomach gratify its yearning to be touched. My hands followed the shape of her arse, then thrust themselves down into her trousers. She, too, wore no pants and I could soon feel the hot, tense globes and filled my hands with them, with slow sensuality. She said 'Shall we sit down?' and took me to where several cushions placed together against the wall made a sort of low sofa. We sat side by side and she leaned over me, to cajole my erection into increasing its dimensions under the silky covering, while I undid her trousers and felt hair and soft skin inside. This process of intrusion, and touching without seeing, aroused us both, as our breathing betrayed. When I found the slit beneath the hair, it was humid, and seemed to seize my fingers as they wriggled their way in. I became obsessed by the urge to see what I felt, yet her layers of clothing meant that a slow ritual undressing lay between me and this prize. She initiated it, by untying the front of my jacket. She fell to kissing my nipples, provoking a sudden, burning desire in me to take her there and then. Her wet lips strayed over the skin stretched under the arch of my ribs, where their slightest touch sent arrows of lust darting through my whole body. As she began to lick me there, leaving a damp snail's trail as her tongue passed, I undid the buttons on the ruffled shirt and her breasts, freed from their straight-jacket, fell ripely into my hands. Although not large, they were full and pear-shaped, with unusually big, upstanding nipples, and I pumped them in my hands and felt their fullness growing as I aroused her. Soon our retreat from the civilised world of decent dress became a rout: she undid my skirt and pulled it down. Then with slow care she released each suspender and rolled down my stockings, stroking the full length of my legs and feet as she did so, and finally pulled off the belt – although for an instant she let its elastic rest on my cock, compressing that unruly member momentarily – though it stood up all the straighter afterwards.

While she was stripping me thus, I tugged at the man's belt on her loose trousers and undid the buttons, and was at last free to fondle her thighs and her cunt without hindrance. But still I wanted to feast my eyes, so I made her stand up and take off everything except the ruffles which made her look so rakish. Then I could see the perfection of her model's body with its pale tan against which the large dark nipples stood out dramatically. They seduced my mouth at once, and I attached myself to them, milking one then the other like a greedy baby, while her hands took hold of my cock and rolled it between them. She had a way of pulling the foreskin back which made me feel deliciously exposed, and when she bent her head and began to lick the naked gland and her saliva bathed its pulsing globe, I lay back to savour the bliss, hands behind my head. Her appetite for my cock seemed inexhaustible, for she chewed and sucked at it for what seemed like hours, grazing the tenderest part with her teeth as if to warn me that she was a carnivore under the skin, while she weighed and measured my balls in her hands, provoking rival sensations in those two pleasure centres. I felt replete, but could have watched her banqueting for ever. At last, however, she straightened up and said, 'Let's go to bed.'

The bedroom was stark by contrast with her crowded, colourful sittingroom. Painted warm orange, it contained nothing but a huge, circular bed and a small bedside cabinet in white wood. She drew down a blind and switched on a muted light which painted our bodies a warm shade of peach. Then she took off her shirt and lay down on the bed, wearing only her bow tie, and held out her arms to me. I discarded my shimmering jacket and lay down beside her. By this stage both of our bodies were supercharged with desire, burning to graft themselves on to each other. We embraced, and rolled this way and that, pressing ourselves together. Her skin was soft and yielding. I clamped her buttocks in my hands and writhed against her, squeezing my prick tight against her belly where its massive hardness seemed to drive her wild, making her thrash about. She too sought my buttocks once more, and opened them again and then, with no preliminary exploration, she suddenly drove a finger down the mysterious passage of my arse, brutally forcing it through the tight hole. It felt like rape, and I shivered with shock, but my cock responded by bounding joyously against her. As her finger probed deeper and seemed to reach my innermost depths, the sensation was devastating. My cock became secondary – indeed, I almost forgot it existed. All my lust was suddenly concentrated inside my violated arse, which she tickled and tormented until it felt explosive. But her fingers dammed the passage and pent up my sensation. I forget what I was doing to her – I think my hands were in her cunt – but my consciousness had expelled all else except this deliciously indecent assault.

My disappointment when she stopped was boundless but, when that overwhelming, piercing pleasure had ceased, the sensation returned to the rest of my numbed body and my prick stirred tumultuously between us.

'Now, for that, I shall fuck you senseless,' I threatened.

'It's high time for your revenge,' she said, 'but first I have something for you.'

What could it be? I wondered. She reached into the drawer of the bedside cupboard and drew out a small object. When she showed it to me, I saw only a hollow cylinder of hard, black rubber, perhaps four inches long and two-and-a-half in diameter.

'What's it for?' I asked warily.

'Can't you guess?' was her reply as she slipped it over my cock. 'Now try to fuck me.'

Although the cylinder fitted it very loosely, I was stimulated by the awareness of the restriction on my cock's activities and intrigued by the device. I wondered if fucking would still be possible. To achieve the greatest depth of penetration, I lifted her legs over my shoulders.

Her hair had come loose from its knot and was spread over the pillow, and I saw at last the classic beauty of her face, which urged me on to possess her. Her cunt was open and waiting for me, with its enigmatic lips parted and its dark portal begging for a rude invasion. Constantly aware of the rubber sleeve which hampered my movements, I tried to get inside her. The first inch was easy, and I found a succulent, clinging surface surrounding the tip of my cock. I eased in another inch, into that hot tropic, and found myself brought up short by the rigid rubber. So this was the game! I could move in and out freely, but only to a depth of an inch or two. The obstacle and the frustration excited me. As I began to set up a rhythm of entry and withdrawal, which was all I could do, her breathing became heavy, matching my rhythm. Of course – for her I was providing the strongest sensation possible, since the inside walls of the vagina are virtually nerveless, and all the nerves cluster at the entrance. From the woman's viewpoint, why ever bother with full penetration? But the device was more than a perverse feminist instrument of torture, for the ultra-sensitive end of my cock could still penetrate her as it wished and please itself. As the tension built up between our legs, I knew that this was another example where the part is greater than the whole.

I thrust away as far as my rubber gaoler permitted, and she was panting, and clawing my back incontinently. The partial stimulation, the thrust which always stopped short just inside the entrance to her cunt aroused her more than any full-blooded fuck could ever have done, and I felt her body stiffen. I too was teased beyond endurance by her trick, and each time that I moved I felt that if I could get in a little deeper the next time, I'd be

147

there. I tried other movements and directions to extract that last ounce of stimulation needed to bring myself off – forgetting about her altogether. I withdrew and wiped my wet tip across the surface of her cunt, then up and down between the labia, thrilling her clitoris with this direct pressure, so that she called out with pleasure. Then I entered her again, and half-fucked her with a slow, regular motion. My strokes, although shallow, were forceful and deliberate and this soon brought her once more to that pre-orgasmic moment when a woman's body becomes hot and flushed pink, but shivers as if with cold. Then I felt her great, uncontrollable contractions and all her tension dissolved as she came with shouts of delight. This was enough for me: careless of whether I broke the rules of her game, I whipped off the rubber gaoler which had so restricted my access and sank into her still throbbing cunt as far as I could. This sudden sense of totality weakened my will to prolong my pleasure, and after only a few strokes which went right up inside her, I cried out like a madman and crazily spilled out my soul.

Chloe seemed not exhausted but refreshed by her fulfilment, and brought me another glass of whisky and sat chatting to me about Paris while we shared it. With her straight hair hanging over her shoulders, her comic bow tie skewed round to one side, she was a magnificent creature – why do such women need to become whores? Then she said she had to pack and catch a train, so I hastily went to the bathroom and dressed. When I returned, she was already wearing another costume – black satin dungarees with a scarlet blouse, which exaggerated the long lines of her splendid figure. I desired her all over again, but she was bent over her suitcase,

148

throwing garments randomly into it, so I said I would go, and wished her '*Bon voyage*'. We shook hands as we parted. 'You would make a lovely woman!' she said to me as I left.

Country Pleasures

Once more I cursed the conventions of the situation, which prevented my ever making a date to see one of the prostitutes again. Not that I had any reason to think they felt the same, but I certainly yearned to meet Chloe once more, and the garden-nymph – and most of all, Chantal. Instead, I found the perpetual Virginie in my room, setting out my lunch. She burst out laughing as she saw me, showing large, hungry teeth. 'What is it?' I asked crossly.

'Monsieur, or rather *Mademoiselle*, should look at herself in the glass.'

I did so at once, and saw that my face was still heavily made-up, but that the eye-black had got smeared during our passionate lovemaking, and now surrounded my eyes in great circles, making me not the glamorous transvestite I had once been, but a staring owl. I washed, scrubbing myself roughly, and my old face was restored at last, but by this time cheeky Virginie had gone. Often

I wished that she would tell me my programme in advance: the uncertainty as to when my services would next be required kept me constantly on edge, unable to enjoy the prospect of the next orgy, or to feel in total control of my life and body. But this too was probably deliberate – and prostitutes themselves must feel similarly undetermined. A revelation came to me: over the past few days I had, more and more, felt myself unconsciously in the role of a prostitute, to be summoned and dismissed as necessary. Now my conscious brain formulated that this is just what I was, no mistake. The perception of myself as unpaid gigolo servicing so many whores pleased me by its irony. Although they made me work, at least they fed me properly! I sat down to eat my lunch ravenously.

Since the weather was sunny again after the storms, I decided to walk in the country, taking my notebook. As I went down the drive and crossed the threshold through the great gates, it seemed that I had been locked up in this house for ever. I relished the sight of the fields and the retreating horizon, even though nobody could have called the view scenic. For some reason, my feet impelled me towards the village, perhaps in the hope of seeing a soul not held in thrall by the big house. As always, the place was deserted, but I saw a bulldozer at work, turning over the soil in the garden of one of the newest bungalows. I speculated on which of the girls it might belong to. The gardens of the older houses looked well-tended and were bright with roses and other summer flowers. But today not even a washing-line gave any hint of occupation. I walked beyond the village along the road to the main town, and turned off into a pasture full of long grass, buttercups and aromatic weeds, where I stretched out on the earth, which the hot sun had already dried.

It was hard to see how I should begin to codify my most recent adventures. The symbolism of today's transvestism was straightforward, but that of the garden scene last night was more elusive. That word gave me the clue.

ELUSIVENESS: Perhaps because of a long history of pursuit and submission, wooing and winning, the female sex incorporates acts of elusion into its sexual fantasies. An alternative explanation may well be that, in the face of the physical power of the stronger sex, the female's only recourse is to flight. (I was thinking of the hide-and-seek among the trees.) Flight becomes ritualised in the fantasy, when there is no question that the woman wants to evade her pursuer permanently – quite the opposite. The act of flight is in itself an act of seduction. But it is not quite so simple as this: in everyday life, when man and woman are in a situation in which fantasy may or may not be operating, how is the male to know whether or not the woman's elusiveness is capricious, or in earnest? In some cases, we may speculate, the female does not even know herself. In an unambiguously fantastic context, the purpose of elusion is *illusion*. (I could not resist this pleasing inaccuracy.) The male fears that he may not be gratified after all, and the woman thus sharpens both his appetite and her own by her evasive tactics.

So what? I wondered if this was not just purposeless word-spinning; but I knew that my own fantasies, or those of the men I knew, rarely featured elusion. Indeed, one of their preconditions seemed invariably to be the premature seizure of the object of desire, so this difference must somehow be significant. But for the present I found myself in a cul-de-sac. As I contemplated my next foray into the female mysteries, my attention was attracted by a car passing along the unfrequented road. It was a huge green Peugeot saloon with an open sun-roof and, as far as I could make out, a woman at the wheel. It disappeared into the village and the sound of its engine faded and was obliterated by the humming of insects about my head.

This pleasant and natural setting led me to think of what I had discovered the previous morning about the special proximity of women to nature. Of course, the events of last night had provided ample evidence for the tribal superstitions on this subject. The girl darting between the trees so gracefully had seemed in perfect accord with her surroundings – unity with nature? No wonder that the spirits of trees and rivers in ancient mythology are always female – the affinities between a woman's body and such natural objects are undeniable, bewitching. Last night I, on the other hand, had felt staid, baffled and uneasy among all those growing things, and the cosmic spectacle of the storm. Again, I could draw no conclusions; the girl last night was young and boundlessly energetic – she would have been equally at ease on the disco dance-floor as in that garden. That one instance could not really form the basis of a theory of Modern Woman's Attunement to Natural Forces – what a pity! As I mentally riffled through my most recent experiences I was struck forcibly by something which seemed to be unique in each case but which, when the cases were aggregated, constituted a Trend. The sociologist in me thrilled to this discovery. I wrote

SUBJUGATION OF THE PHALLUS: Whatever the rights or wrongs of the Freudian account of penis envy, most women are indisputably fascinated by the male member, and in fantasy their treatment of it is far more imaginative than the male's almost invariably direct and narcissistic approach to his own phallus. The woman's intention, as far as it can be interpreted – and any interpretation of fantasy is, of course, questionable – is to restrict, impede or in some other way subjugate the erect phallus and bend it to her will. (I had before me three different sources of evidence for this hypothesis: the bandaging of my cock by Chantal, the cage, now packed away in my valise, and the rubber cylinder which had afforded Chloe so much satisfaction.) As with elusiveness, the intention is not totally serious, and the woman would doubtless be vexed if the phallus responded to her treatment by becoming flaccid, or if she subjugated it so successfully as to prevent penetration. The form which this subconscious desire to subjugate takes in fantasy is usually as follows: the woman wraps the erect penis in some tight-fitting glove or other device which makes penetration, or even movement, impossible. Very often the tip is allowed to protrude. However, the woman, having done this, does not transfer her attention to another part of the man's anatomy, but redoubles her attention to the phallus – *reculer pour mieux sauter*?

Her treatment of the imprisoned instrument, which in some contexts represents to her menace and violation, is often teasing, as if her intention were to annihilate by ridicule this potential disturbance or threat to her mental and bodily equilibrium. When we consider the way in which in our culture, mothers epitomise the penis to their daughters as an instrument of shame (loss of virginity, pregnancy, etc.) and violence (rape), it is not surprising that female fantasy takes this form and defuses the threat symbolically, but it would be instructive to study the treatment of the phallus by women in cultures where polygamy or free love prevail. It must also be admitted that this desire to conceal, restrict, tease and, in general, *play with* the penis might merely be another manifestation of the childish desire to manipulate anything protuberant; likewise, men's fascination with breasts (*vide* PROTUBERANCES).

I felt I was getting somewhere at last! But my concentrated effort had emptied my mind, and the idea of walking slowly back through the heavy, still mid-afternoon heat appealed to me now. Nevertheless, to complete the record, I made a few notes on role reversal, alias transvestism, although these dwelt mainly on my own reactions to the experience, and were for my personal interest. I still had little idea what Chloe had got out of it, for she had not tried to dominate me, or in any way caricature a dyke, despite her butch appearance. But, I reflected, she seemed to enjoy herself.

Getting to my feet, I strolled back through the village. The bulldozer driver was sitting down against a sunny wall, enjoying a Gitane, and I recognised him as the odd-job man and waved, but he showed no inclination to come and speak to me, so I went on. Stepping back through the gates seemed for an instant like the descent into the Inferno, so liberated and fancy-free had I felt sitting in that heady meadow. But I knew at heart that I could not leave the place until I had drunk my fill of all that was offered to me. As I came up the drive to the lawn, I saw the green Peugeot parked ostentatiously on the gravel, just outside the house. Another new arrival – my mind was instantly full of conjectures. The windows of my room were open and it was flooded with scented air from the garden; everything looked so orderly that I suspected Virginie of having done some invisible cleaning – and perhaps having explored my suitcases into the bargain.

As there was still some time before dinner, I resorted once again to canned entertainment, and switched on my private television circuit. At last I saw what I had been longing to see for the past two days, the magic cat, Chantal. Filming had begun before I arrived, because she stood in her bedroom in patched jeans and a loose T-shirt, that made her look like some street urchin. The cat's mask lay on the bed. She stretched up her arms and pulled off her T-shirt and I was thrilled by the sight of those budding breasts, erupting from her straight body. I could not resist opening my flies and I masturbated instinctively as I watched the scene unfold. She took down her jeans, and there was the complete, naked, unmasked girl that I had never seen. Then she put on the mask hastily and went to the door with the silk scarf in her hand. The sequence that followed was familiar to me and proved almost more exciting, carefully edited, than the real events which it recorded. When I saw the rampant evil demon bend her over and take her in front of the mirror, I jerked myself off with indescribable, vicarious pleasure. Just at that moment, inevitably, Virginie passed by the open window and, pausing to look in, witnessed my frantic climax. Unlike most peeping Toms, she did not pretend to have seen nothing, but remained framed in the open window, her mouth open in a carefully composed expression of surprise, long enough for me to notice her before going on. Was nothing sacred here? I was irked, perhaps unjustifiably since, as my governess might have admonished me, people who masturbate in front of open windows must expect to be caught.

The pattern of the video recordings was well-established by now. Some scene from my own escapades would be followed by a piece of antique commercial erotica, courtesy of Eros Films Inc., or vice versa. The next sequence began very innocently. A man and a woman, seen from a distance, were sitting at a game of chess which must just have begun, for the board still had its full contingent of pieces. The young woman's face was pretty, Fay Wray-style, with that vacant expression which girls seem to wear before they find their feet in the world. Her hair was fair and crimped and she had plump cheeks, wide vulnerable eyes and a Cupid's bow mouth with dark lipstick. The young man was a far less pleasing specimen. His face was unshaven, sullen and rapacious, with something anthropoid about it. He looked like a gorilla stuffed into a man's suit. Every so often, he looked slyly at his companion out of the corner of his eyes. She opened the game, he replied to her gambit, and so it went on for a few minutes until the girl lost her first pawn. The man smiled triumphantly and gestured to her and she reluctantly started to take off the beaded over-blouse which she was wearing. Underneath, she wore a figured silk blouse, with pearls and a scarf knotted loosely at the neck. It was impossible to see what she was wearing below, because of the table. As the game proceeded, it became clear that the unprepossessing ape was almost a champion compared with his partner. Although he lost his knight soon after, and took off his tie, the girl lost two more pieces, pawn and rook, in quick succession, and scarf and pearls were tossed away. Now she was down to her blouse. The game became tenser and the gaps between moves were more protracted, as if each knew how much depended on it. Another of the young man's pieces was captured – I thought he sacrificed it deliberately – and he removed his belt with a suggestive smile.

Now an elaborate castling manoeuvre took place – unwisely on the woman's part, it seemed, because she ended by losing her bishop. She looked pleadingly at her uncouth opponent and asked him something, but he shook his head and, very slowly, she unbuttoned her blouse and took it off. He affected to be absorbed in the play and not to notice the sight on the other side of the table, but I saw him sneaking glances surreptitiously. Underneath the blouse she was wearing some kind of old-fashioned satin vest, which hung loosely around her breasts. Decency, for the moment, was preserved. But not for long because, although the man now lost a pawn and removed his jacket, he had his revenge one move later when he took her queen. He seemed to be telling her, by his gestures, that such a powerful piece was worth two items of clothing, but she shook her head obstinately, and unbuttoned the modesty vest. As soon as she had taken it off, she crossed her arms defensively across her chest – but not before I, and her opponent, had the chance to see the delightful, tiny, egg-shaped breasts which stood out almost horizontally.

As she played, she now leaned forward to hide her shame, and eventually she succeeded in taking the black bishop. Apparently there were no rules governing the order in which garments were to be removed, for the man stood up and let down his trousers. She looked away in genuine modesty, but the viewer could see – since he wore no underpants – the monstrous erection of a cock developed out of all proportion to his body. His unpleasant face was shining with sweat and contorted with lewd excitement, but he sat down again at once, to complete his inevitable victory on the chess board. Another white rook was lost, then several more white pieces, and the loser wriggled furiously about in her chair, evidently taking off stockings and skirt under the table, although the camera's angle hid this process from the viewer. She had now lost so many pieces that she could only hope to defend herself – and barely that – and had lost all hope of capturing any more black pieces.

The man's eyes wandered more and more from the game, across the table to where his opponent's arms still sheltered her body, and under the table, where his own hands were busy. But he finally recalled his attention to the game for long enough to check, then checkmate, her in a corner of the board. Metaphorically too, she was mated. She looked crestfallen and fearful, but a lecherous grin was lighting up his face. He told her to get up – she demurred. He shouted at her bullyingly (or so I guessed, since the movie was entirely silent) and she got up and very slowly lowered her satin knickers, revealing a small, sculpted mound dusted lightly with curling fair hair. She could not conceal both her breasts and this new

160

disgrace simultaneously, so she elected to put her hands where her fig-leaf should have been. He came round the table to her, still half-clothed in his shirt, and she started back in horror when she saw the huge cock which preceded him, waving horizontally like a great flag. She abandoned all modesty, and hid her face in her hands. But he pulled them away and, pointing to the floor, made her lie on it, face downwards.

Without hesitation, he forced her legs apart – encountering fierce resistance, it appeared – and knelt down between them, preparing to assault her with his awesome bludgeon. I bit my lip, so real did this horrible fiction seem. At the tense moment when his prick came up against the resistance of her sealed cunt, and he was preparing to force himself in with his hands with brutal haste, he was suddenly distracted. He looked over to his right. The camera switched to a corner of the room where a door opened and several girls in Charleston-style dresses rushed in. They ran over and grabbed the man, shouting and gesticulating. They slapped his face and pulled him across the table, and started to beat him soundly with the belt which he had taken off so gleefully. One girl went over to the defeated chess-player, who had got up and was dressing, and put her arms round her. 'It's all right,' she seemed to be saying 'Come and take your revenge!' The Fay Wray lookalike cheered up, went over to the table and took the belt. The film closed with a shot of the chessboard, its pieces overturned and rolling to the floor. For some reason, the title of the film was shown at the end. It was 'Injured Innocence'.

This strange fable nauseated me almost as much as Dr Lalande's stories the previous evening and I vowed to analyse why, as soon as I had leisure to think. But I was reminded that it was nearly time to go and meet the macabre and loquacious doctor for dinner – an event which I was not much looking forward to. When I arrived in the dining room, Madame and Lalande were already sipping champagne and they made me welcome. The conversation once again revolved around the elite social circle to which they both evidently belonged. Then it turned to recent medical scandals: limbs accidentally amputated, and suchlike. Madame did not seem to object to the bloody nature of her physician's narratives, but I suspected that she was slightly bored, and her eyes kept straying towards me, as if inviting me to intervene and cut short the flow. As we sat down to a plate of excellent devilled fish, Lalande engaged me in a conversation which suggested that he too had been watching the closed-circuit television.

'Do you find in your analysis, Monsieur Smith, that it is possible to draw a boundary line between fantasy and perversion?'

'In principle I suppose it's possible, but not so easy in practice. It rather depends on the so-called perversion. What did you have in mind?'

'Well – *transvestism*, for example.'

'Would you really call that a perversion? I would have thought it was all a matter of degree.'

'I believe that clinically it is described as perversion – though I am not a psychiatrist, of course.'

Remembering how I had enjoyed this perversion that same morning, I was moved to defend it more staunchly than I would have done a few days back.

'It seems to me that transvestism, in most of its manifestations, is no more than an attempt to experience the opposite sex-role, something which our culture denies us in everyday life. Surely it is society that is at fault for drawing such strict boundaries between the sexes, not the individuals who wish to cross them?'

Madame interposed. 'But that assumes a lot. In effect you are denying, Monsieur Smith, that there are any *natural* sex-roles. If there are, then the attempt to transgress them is surely unnatural – or perverse, as the doctor puts it.'

I intuited that this seasoned feminist was secretly on my side of the debate and only played the devil's advocate to increase her dinner-time amusement. Before making my reply, I helped myself to a large portion of the *cuisses de grenouille* that Virginie had just deposited on the table, my favourite dish in the whole of French cuisine. Then I struggled to explain myself better.

'I certainly admit that there are a few basic differentiations between the sexes which rest on their biological differences. It's what Marx and Engels called 'the sexual division of labour'. But what I'm arguing is that a culture can reinforce and exaggerate them to make them seem permanent – or else eliminate them entirely. For example, a society that collectivises the rearing of children and takes the infant from its mother abolishes one of the most important determinants of her social sex-role. And if we could perfect the production of babies in jam-jars, as Huxley imagines in *Brave New World*, there would not need to be any social sex distinctions at all; the only noticeable and inevitable sex difference would be during the sex act.'

'Is that what you would advocate, then, Monsieur?' Lalande asked, with a touch of irony.

'Well – perhaps not wholly. I think that the socially

163

constructed differences between the sexes make for variation and exciting tensions – and, sexually speaking, for greater pleasure.'

'Such as transvestism, the contravention of the differences!' he concluded triumphantly.

'Why not? But I still don't think that "perversion" is the right label for such a fantasy. As with sadism, it only becomes a perversion if the man or woman is neurotically obsessed with it, unable to relate to the partner in any other way.' I was keen to try out this new theory of mine on a medical man. Lalande was delicately holding a frog's leg between his sensitive fingers looking at it as if contemplating major surgery. He seemed unimpressed.

'There is something in what you say. But let me tell you a story which was recounted to me by a colleague. He had two patients, a happily married couple as far as he knew, although the woman had always seemed rather masculine to him. She informed him that she was four months pregnant and asked for a check-up. When he came to examine her, he found that far from being pregnant, she was in fact a *man*, the effeminate half of this gay couple. They were desperately keen to adopt a child, and had arranged this privately with a young mother-to-be. While awaiting the birth of the baby, the "woman" not only simulated pregnancy but even, she claimed, suffered symptoms such as nausea. This outlandish case suggests to me that what starts as role-borrowing, if you choose to call it that, ends up as full-scale perversion – sickness!'

'Perhaps that illustrates the unusual case of neurotic obsession that I mentioned,' I agreed, adding, 'but it seems to me that the fault lies in the society which dictates that we adopt either one role or the other. Why

164

shouldn't a maternal homosexual foster a child if he wants to, without going through such a palaver? Since both sexes share male and female hormones to some degree, everyone is bound to want to cross the cultural role-boundaries sometimes. You have merely given an extreme example which is sad, rather than perverse.'

Here, Madame interrupted our monotonous dialogue.

'Neither of you really understands the woman's point of view – how could you? Because our culture attaches all the trappings of power, wealth and prestige to the male role, it is perfectly *natural* for a woman to want to experience the male role and share its benefits – so-called penis envy apart!'

I agreed heartily with this insight, but Lalande said nothing. We moved on to a gateau which was a sensual delight in itself, and I observed Lalande closely. Although he showed no signs of effeminacy, I wondered if his hostility to transvestism might not be self-defensive: people often attack that which they most fear in themselves. Certainly, he was elegant and somewhat affected, but everything about him was redolent of masculine success. I could not help liking the fellow for his gentle manners and envying such assurance. But his presence there still made me nervous.

Madame had evidently decided that the subject should be changed and, like the most diplomatic of hostesses, proceeded to create a diversion.

'Since we have talked so much of female fantasy in the last few days, perhaps I could turn the question round and ask you both what are your favourite fantasies?'

I was put out by such a direct question and replied evasively that, as she already knew, my own overwhelming desire was to participate in women's fantasies; I knew the male genre only too well, and it bored me. Lalande had no such inhibitions about revealing his secret desires.

'All my life,' he replied, 'I have been haunted by a recurrent dream – a waking dream, I should say – in which I am lying asleep in the centre of a great marquee, in an enormous bed. A sound wakes me, and I look round and see the shadows of women against the walls of the tent, moving stealthily towards the entrance. There are three shadows, tall, distorted and immensely sinister. I try to get out of bed, but my limbs are paralysed, powerless to move. Then they enter the marquee; two of them look like savages, dressed only in ragged leopard-skins, with long, knotted hair and fierce faces, but the third woman is older, still beautiful and very dignified, and wears a long evening dress in shimmering colours. She seems to be in authority over the others. They come over to me and pull the covers off the bed and examine my naked body, like butchers inspecting a carcass, poking me with their fingers, and feeling the size of my prick.

'The older woman nods and the two wild ones pick me up by my hands and feet and, slinging me between them, carry me out of the tent. Outside there is a distant fair ground with fireworks shooting off into the night sky, and I can see people milling around some way off. I call out for help, but nobody hears. Then they lay me on the ground and, while the two fur-clad warriors pinion my arms and legs tightly, their leader masturbates me and abuses me in unmentionable ways. Although I am terrified, I am also aroused – stiff with horror, as it were. At last, she pulls up her long skirt, squats over me and thoroughly violates me. Whenever I show signs of

166

excitement, she stops, and one of her minions hits me. Then she takes the place of the woman holding my feet, who pulls open her leopard-skin wrap and has her turn – and then the one at my head, each raping me after her own fashion, swallowing me up in their hard voracious cunts.

'The women never come, but for hours they keep me in such a state of fearful arousal that I suspect them of putting cantharides on my prick – and I too, cannot come, but have to go on and on with the torment of the never-ending ante-climax. Then the dawn breaks and instantly the three ghosts vanish, leaving me on the dewy grass, utterly drained and senseless.'

'How fascinating,' said Madame, feigning distant politeness. But she had shown such interest as he recounted the story that I suspected her of identifying with the authoritarian leader of the ghostly rapists. 'But it sounds more like a dream of torture than a fantasy of sexual gratification.'

'On the contrary, although there is no consummation for me, the sensation of being robbed of my last ounce of sexual strength, against my will, is incomparably satisfying.'

As I steadfastly refused to offer my own sequel to Lalande's fiction, the other two went on to talk of different matters, clearly finding me something of a spoilsport. I thought the fantasy a strange one for a man with Lalande's masculine confidence, but perhaps, I reflected, those with limitless power and self-assurance in everyday life dream of the reverse, of the abdication of responsibility. Maybe the wish-fulfilment dream of a macho man so accustomed to making the running with women, is to have all sexual initiative taken out of his

167

hands, and to become someone else's object. This, at least, was the best interpretation I could concoct. After coffee, Madame looked at her watch and said to me pointedly, 'You are expected in Room 15 any moment now. Have a pleasant evening.'

I remembered that Lalande was leaving the next morning, so I wished him a good journey to Marseilles and said goodbye, although Madame said significantly, 'Perhaps you will meet again.'

Room 15

Room 15 was on the second floor, a green baize door facing the corridor at the far end. It stood ajar, so I went in and found myself in a small lobby, facing three more doors. I knocked at each of them, and, receiving no reply, went through the central door and discovered myself in an Arabian nights setting. The walls were hung with rich oriental tapestries, some attached to the centre of the ceiling and the walls, so that they billowed down forming a false ceiling and making the room seem like the interior of a sheik's tent. Several wide, low couches with fat cushions stood against the wall and the floor was covered with richly patterned eastern rugs, scattered over a fine Persian carpet. I also noticed a number of large mirrors with antique gilt frames, propped up against the walls behind the couches, adding new angles and dimensions to this exotic creation. Outside the window it was nearly dark, but clay lanterns hung around the rooms at different heights and a soft light escaped from their intricately carved holes. I wondered where in this motley, lavish room the camera was concealed.

I heard a sound behind me and a soft voice said 'I am at your service, master.' When I turned, there was an oriental phantom behind me – someone dressed in full Islamic *hejab*, complete with the veil. All I could see of her was a hint of sparkling eyes behind the net-covered slit in her head-dress and, when I looked down, naked feet hung heavily with gold ankle-bracelets. An Arab? The white slave trade reversed? Sometimes the alacrity of my imagination pleases me: I acted my part perfectly. I sprawled at full length on one of the couches and said, 'Take off my shoes and bring me a drink.' Silently, she obeyed both commands, and knelt by the couch, massaging my feet as I sipped iced rum and Coke. I asked for music and she turned on a cassette player from which issued the sounds of an endless Persian love-song, with the wavering woman's voice wailing its arbitrary notes in dialogue with the precise, mechanical orchestra of flutes and strange strings. The sad, indeterminate tune evoked in me unspeakable nostalgia for the East – and for her women. After I had listened in silence for some time, the veiled figure spoke again. 'Can I do something else for you, master?' A request which was somehow a rebuke for my inner preoccupation.

'Yes. Remove my clothes and give me a body massage – with plenty of oil.'

I had no doubt at all that she would have oil near at hand because I felt, more strongly even than during the past week, that the fantasy was acting in me, not I acting the fantasy, however impromptu and original my commands sounded to me as I issued them. Silent and submissive once more, she undressed me as I lay there. I saw fine, smooth-skinned hands which were so pale and creamy that they must belong to an Arab princess, I thought. From a round, inlaid table in the centre of the room she took a small vial, filled with golden oil. My guess that this fantasy was lacking in no detail had been right. I shut my eyes and the music droned plaintively on, while I felt cool oil pouring on to my chest and light hands gliding over my body. A heavy smell of sandalwood filled my nostrils. She began at my neck and shoulders and then moved downwards, first teasing my outer skin into awareness with a featherlike touch. After that, she moved into the second stage of the massage and began kneading my chest and stomach with such accurate strength that every inch of my body responded with wincing delight, except my cock, which so far she had ignored. I knew intuitively that she had reserved this for a final, esoteric ritual massage, and I was more than content to wait for the anticipated delights to unfold at the hands of my self-proclaimed slave.

My legs and feet were massaged with equally loving care, affording a sensation even more exquisite than the morning stretch after getting out of bed. Now only one area was left untouched, which cried out for her attention, and stiffened in expectation of her touch. But now hands were under my ribs, rolling me over, and she started work on my back. The same agreeable stroking, squeezing and pounding motions now began again, moving up inside my thighs, which made me shiver with delight, over my buttocks – another avid focus of pleasure – and up my back until every joint of my spine ached pleasantly with the relentless pressure. Some people maintain that massage is intrinsically sexy, but I find it affords a different, more relaxed pleasure than the raging thirst which other caresses provoke. What is without parallel is the use of massage as a prelude to better things – in expectation of which my appetite was sharpened and pricked me everywhere. Again, her skilful hands turned me over and replenished themselves with oil. This she smoothed over my cock which filled itself beneath her touch and rested heavily in her hands as she encouraged and provoked it to swell up like a balloon. Some of the oil trickled over my balls, and she kneaded it into them, this way and that, contracting her hands as if to squeeze their juice out, while my cock rose high in the air, clamouring for her attention again. While her hands moulded me like plastic, bending me to her whims, I kept my eyes closed, which served to focus the bliss more sharply wherever her hands passed. She took my cock again and jigged it constantly until I was so full and potent I feared to burst in her hands. So I opened her eyes and shouted at her to stop at once.

'I want to see your body. Undress yourself,' I ordered sharply, my voice giving no hint of how much she had pleased me.

I never discovered how those shapeless robes fastened, but she seemed to unpeel them from the back, and they fell from her shoulders, revealing a pale body of such incomparable, womanly voluptuousness that I caught my breath. I could not have guessed that beneath the robes which drowned her she would be so petite, so fresh and untouched. Her hips were full and lyre-shaped and above her tiny waist were two white breasts of such perfect, fat roundness as I had never seen before. The pink, pointed nipples at their centres were the finishing point of this divine creation, the point of entry to that

172

flawless flesh. I wanted to detach those plump breasts from her body and juggle them in my hands. Below the pale expanse of her elliptical belly was a tiny cluster of golden hairs which reminded me of the sweet promise of her cunt. I could hardly wait to violate that perfection – I even hoped that she might be a virgin so that I could savour the rupture of her barred passage, the soiling of the innocent.

'And now take off your veil.'

When she did this I saw, with a thrill of recognition, the extravagant gold curls of the girl whose arrival had so distracted me on Sunday. Her porcelain face wore an expression of humble submission to my will, her blue eyes were downcast, scarcely visible beneath the fringed lashes, but her bow of a mouth seemed to be suppressing a smile.

'Now lie on top of me. I want to take my pleasure,' I decreed. Inwardly I craved to feel the weight of that seductive body on mine, and her breasts crushed against my yearning nipples. Obedient still, she stepped on to the couch and lay still on top of me. I breathed heavily, while every nerve in my body vibrated at this motion-less contact. She was not heavy, yet her flesh pressed luxuriously on me, and seemed to blend with mine in a long, warm rhapsody. I forced myself to break the spell.

'Now, fuck me like the whore that you are,' I said. I did not trouble to caress her, for her touch on me seemed so complete. And pashas must take care not to exhaust themselves unnecessarily, I remembered, with so many women to satisfy. Scarcely lifting her body from mine, she raised her buttocks and insinuated the fullness of my cock between her legs, into the heart of a cunt so eager to

173

swallow me that I laughed with sheer delight. She fucked me indolently, with movements so slight that I strained to feel them. But friction there was, between those soft, sucking surfaces, and it fanned a wild, hot flame in my loins which all the moisture inside her could not quench. My head was turned to the wall, my eyes shut again, and my consciousness had migrated from there to the throbbing lower parts of my body, when it was suddenly recalled by the sound of a door opening. I opened my eyes and saw, in the mirror which I faced, Lalande standing in the doorway, naked as God intended except for a heavy gold belt, encrusted with stones, low on his hips. His tall figure was muscled but not heavy, and his black skin shc⁻e. A magnificent heathen in this temple of Eros. He spoke to me, almost obsequiously.

'Is the whore behaving properly? Is she satisfactory? Is her cunt sweet enough?'

My versatile imagination adapted quickly to this unwelcome interruption. 'She is very unsatisfactory – much too lazy and sluggish. And she has forgotten to refill my glass.'

'Get up, woman, and fetch us two more glasses,' said Lalande, and she extricated herself from my embrace and shuffled off with downcast head, while Lalande stood domineeringly in the centre of the room, admiring himself in a mirror. I rarely have the chance to see another man's naked body – the boys in the shower-room at school were quite a different species of human life – so inevitably I looked curiously at his prick, which hung between his legs, a thick, dark cylinder, swollen but not yet erect. In some circumstances his inopportune appearance would have threatened me intolerably, but I felt that we were actors in the same, predetermined play, whose roles were so clearly demarcated that neither of us need feel any rivalry. For his part, he appraised my body with equal interest, but said nothing. The girl, still dragging her feet, brought back two goblets and gave one to each of us, then stood, head bent, in front of Lalande. He drank thirstily, then said 'And now, for your slothfulness, you will be beaten.' He took off the gilded leather belt and motioned her to lie on a couch, then began to beat her across the buttocks – not too heavily, I thought, but as the wide leather slapped across her flesh she gave a series of sharp, animal cries. After twenty strokes, he invited me to take my revenge, and, seizing the belt from him, I began to lay into her arse, almost violently in my desire to defile her perfection. Her buttocks were as voluptuous as her breasts, two soft, full curves protruding beneath her shapely waist, but now they were striped with pink weals. Her flesh heaved and she writhed, raising up her angel's arse to meet each new chastisement, and the sharp sound of leather cracking against flesh filled the room and punctuated the interminable love-song. My lust was stirred again by this indirect contact and I held my prick in one hand as I delivered singeing strokes with the other. Lalande stood frowning at her, and when I had run out of energy, he completed her punishment by slapping her arse hard with his bare hands – for his own satisfaction, I guessed.

He turned to me again and asked, 'Has she been punished enough?'

'Not yet, considering how negligent she has been.'

'What shall I do to the slut next?'

Almost against my will, certainly against my better

judgement, I replied 'Fuck her like a snake – fuck her unconscious.'

As if he had expected this reply, he promptly made her open her legs. For him, no preparation was needed, for his cock bounded up in a savage erection as I spoke. Then he was on top of her and inside her with one quick thrust, and he pounded her so vigorously that I thought she would break in two with his sledge-hammer blows. He crouched behind her and leant on his straightened arms, which pressed down on her shoulders, to get the maximum force into his movements. The mirrors of the room flung back his image at me – the tensely rippling muscles of his dark back, and his intense, war-like face as he fucked her harder and faster, while she shuddered under his impact and gasped out inaudible pleas for him to stop. So enthralled was I by this live theatre of a genre I had never seen before, even in my tours of Sweden, that I was disappointed when his body stopped its rapid drive and he turned back to me and asked deferentially, 'Is she fucked enough? Her cunt's running dry.'

'The sow deserves more than that,' I said, and detected a shiver of pleasure running through her flattened body. A certain childish instinct got the better of me. 'Turn her over, she must be tickled.'

Together we set about tickling her malleable, squirming flesh; he sat on her legs and feet and his dark hands teased their way round her bush and into her cunt, tormenting her clitoris so wickedly that she cried out in apparent anguish. At the same time, I pinned her arms behind her head with one hand and my other strayed randomly over her undulating heaving breasts, sometimes lightly, sometimes pinching folds of skin as

176

hard as I could. Her nipples renewed my desire to tease and I brushed my fingers over them so fleetingly that they seemed to protrude further and further in the effort to reach my hands and be fondled. Soon they were gorged with blood, stiff and deep pink, an open invitation to my mouth. So, by way of variation, I tickled them with my tongue which caused her to shake ecstatically, while my hand played over her belly, dwelling on those sensitive inches at the groin where the merest touch evokes a wincing reflex. My hands brushed against Lalande's black hands as they delved between her white legs, and long black fingers poked into those parts of her that were private no longer, and had become our plaything. Our joint attentions, this wholesale plundering of her sensations, wrought her to the point where she cried out 'Mercy' – meaning, I divined, a breathing space to come down from her plateau of excitement before climbing to even higher levels . Or was it '*Merci*'?

By common, silent consent, Lalande and I took our glasses over to another couch and sat watching her, talking of brothels in the near East (with which he seemed at least as familiar as I) where a customer can have ten women at once, and stretching out our naked bodies pleasurably, side by side. I felt far easier with him now in our equal state of exposure than during our earlier meetings, and was irresistibly drawn to him, for his fine body and the spirit with which he acted his part of punitive servitor. He too seemed to be attracted by me and had we not been dutifully inhabiting the girl's fantasy, we might well have been tempted to inaugurate one of our own. But intuitively I knew that this would be forbidden by the strict code of behaviour in that house, so I merely took visual pleasure in the sight of Lalande, and he shamelessly did the same with me.

The girl, emptied by our combined onslaught, took some time to recover, then she rolled over, leaned upon one elbow and asked meekly if there was anything we required. 'Just come here and give me a rub,' said Lalande, his tone of voice making it clear where she was expected to rub him. She came and, kneeling on the floor in front of us, took a prick in each hand and wondrously revived our flagging spirits with a technique which seemed to combine stroking, squeezing and twisting in one fluent movement. She worked away between us like a mechanical doll, her golden curls obscuring her face, but the sight of that hair falling on her graceful, angular shoulders tugged at my heart. However, there was no room for such sentiment in our male conspiracy. We lounged back, relishing her abject servitude, and continuing with a carefree conversation about his last trip to England and the whores he had met in Soho. We spoke in English, to exclude the girl from our elevated level. At last, satiated with the passive delight which her hands offered, I wanted action.

'The girl is an indolent trollop,' I declared, and Lalande agreed. 'This time what she gets will serve her right. She'll beg us to stop,' he added. We carried her over to the widest couch, putting her on her side, then Lalande lay behind her and I stretched out facing her, my mouth at her throat, my hands covering her breasts. I felt a violent shudder run through her, and guessed that Lalande had forced her from behind, and I could feel the erratic movement of her hips as his energy raced through her, down that small channel which distils each sensation into liquid fire. Her lips moved and she whispered to me, 'You too.' I mouthed back, 'Not possible' but she pleaded, 'Try!' So I insinuated my legs through hers, inevitably tangling them with Lalande's, who scarcely noticed in his absorption in his self-impelled, inward rush. To my surprise, the impossible proved almost easy and I managed to penetrate her and press my cock a good way into her cunt. I began to fuck her slowly, frightened to initiate too violent a movement while that force drove through her arse, lest we damaged her. From the first the multiple benefits of troilism were revealed to me, for through the walls of her cunt I could feel Lalande's prick, and he felt me, and the pumping rhythm which each cock established heightened the sensation of its near neighbour to an extreme of delirium.

The girl's frenzy knew no bounds: while the lower part of her body was firmly anchored between us and filled with a syncopation of movement which echoed through her arse and cunt, the rest of her body jerked about as if possessed by demons – which, in a sense, she was. I envied her passionately, for the rich abundance which she must have been enjoying, yet the throbbing and squeezing which were transmitted to my rampant cock from the passage of her arse were so exquisite, intense and complete that I had nothing left to desire. Eventually, Lalande and I instinctively developed an alternating movement – as he rammed into her, I withdrew, and so on, which kept her continuously filled with our motion – and thus, between us, we took her, as she beat her hands against the pillow and screamed and choked with bestial delight. This exhibition precipitated me into

179

an instant, joyous climax and I felt myself melting inside her and my sperm shot out of me in a wild underground fountain, and I collapsed beside her.

Lalande, impassive as ever, did not come and withdrew when we were finished. He started to put on his gold belt. I looked at him with an unspoken question in my eyes.

'Not for me,' he said. 'Tonight it's her fantasy, and yours. And I have business elsewhere.' He slipped out of the door without another word and I heard his bare feet padding down the corridor – to which room? I wondered vaguely. But he soon disappeared from my memory and I put my arms round the lovely, satiated girl who had captivated me at first sight. Her flesh seemed to glow, its perfection enhanced rather than sullied by our rude defilement. I wanted to be closer to her somehow, so I tried to make her talk.

'Have you ever done that before?' I asked, imagining that the answer would be 'Often'.

'No, it's the first time,' she replied sleepily, 'But from now on I'll do nothing else.'

I felt a pang of regret as I imagined others brutally rending her body, without the gentleness which her fantasy had forced on us.

'Was it like you'd hoped?'

'Far, far better. Such fullness, such bliss . . .' The memory of it flooded over her again and she fell silent. By way of farewell, I took the oil and massaged her erotic body from head to toe: only like this, I felt, could I take possession of her and carry her imprint away in my hands and my mind. She lay making no sound or movement, but she seemed to enjoy my oiled caresses and sighed from time to time. By the time I reached her

180

toes, she was asleep, so I covered her with a blanket, took my clothes and tiptoed away.

Rough Stuff

I did not see Lalande again, though I have often thought of him since. He must have slipped away to catch an early train. But the green Peugeot still stood in front of the house. My breakfast tray was standing on the bedside table when I woke: Virginie must have come in without waking me. The weather was still fine, and I decided to sit in the garden and write. I realised that my stay was drawing to an end and I wanted to record my ideas and experiences as fully as possible before I left that house of magic and the spell was broken irrecoverably. Sitting with my back against the birch tree where the moonlit nymph had stood so tantalisingly, with a warm breeze rustling its leaves, I thought about the night before. I had often been in bed with two women, usually two whores, but I needed to analyse the essential difference between that kind of threesome, so gratifying to the male ego, and what had happened with Lalande and the slave-girl. This morning the words flowed from my pen as if I was inspired.

TROILISM: The quality of this sexual fantasy differs dramatically according to whether the triangle consists of two women and a man or the reverse. In the former case, the fantasy is necessarily male-orientated unless the two women also happen to be lesbians. (This had actually happened to me in Denmark, and I could have written reams about the odd, vicarious pleasure that their delight in each other had afforded me, but I wanted to deal with the more usual case.) In such a situation there are, of course, two orifices and only one phallus to fill them, so that they inevitably compete, objectively speaking, for satisfaction. The man may be energetic and controlled enough to satisfy both women thoroughly, but there will always be one empty orifice. With two men and a woman, by contrast, there are two orifices and two penises, one for each. Thus, all three parties can experience simultaneous satisfaction, but the activity is necessarily orientated towards the woman. Furthermore, since her receptive potential is virtually inexhaustible, the two men can both be sure of gratification. They can also enjoy a variety of pleasures, by alternating between her two passages. The only danger is that the woman may be pleased too quickly by the intensity of the double sensations which shoot through her most sensitive parts, and may come to orgasm and want to stop, but the men can always continue to use her body until they reach their climaxes. The reason why this triangle figures so prominently in women's fantasies (at least, I hoped that it did) must surely be that the simultaneous penetration of all her available orifices affords a feeling of complete plenitude, a delight at which men can only guess. (In the Sadean context, I reflected, a third man would be invoked, who pokes his member into her mouth to ensure that she is corked up, as it were, like a bottle with several necks.)

At a psychological level, there is great satisfaction to be derived from the attentions of two members of the opposite sex – this naturally applies equally to men – and troilistic activity transfers this pleasure to the concrete, physical level. One feature of either kind of triangle is that the minority member, whether male or female, is reduced more absolutely to a sexual object than in any 'normal' sexual practice. This suggests the strength of the conspiracy between the two members of the same sex which the situation sets up, but the object role seems to augment the pleasure of the third party, and his or her feeling of being brought willy-nilly to the point of satiation. (I reflected that last night's whore had manifested this tendency very tangibly by presenting herself from the start as a slave-concubine in the harem setting, but I did not want to bring such personal contingencies into my general argument.)

I asked myself why Lalande, who was so eager to pin the label of perversion on sexual activities, had conceded to take part in this drama, which he must perforce have considered unnatural, destroying as it did the normal balance between the sexes which he advocated. Perhaps, I reflected, his conversation at dinner had only been designed to provoke me, for his own entertainment. In this house I had quickly lost all comprehension of when, whether and how I was being manipulated: on reflection, it seemed to happen all the time! As if to verify this, Virginie now tripped across the lawn to warn me that I was invited to lunch in 'the red room' with Madame Duchamp.

I agreed, of course, but began to long for the moment of my departure when I would once again be an independent agent, free of such demands. Now that my mission was completed, I had no excuse not to return to England. I envisaged the damp green hills which rolled round my country house. The thought of sitting in my study, typing out the manuscript which would distil the essence of all these bizarre events in wise, pungent aphorisms, so allured me that I got up and walked over to the house to find a telephone. I resolved to book a flight for the next afternoon. There was a telephone extension in the dining room, and I soon made the necessary reservation. Then I rang my housekeeper, to warn her of my imminent arrival. Should I ring my old girlfriend? Some instinct warned me against this – after all, who knew what diversions might befall me before my journey had ended? When I arrived I would surprise her. But I found that I was reluctant to think of seeing her again: I did not want to make the old mistake of assuming that my partner's mental development had automatically kept pace with my own, and that she had undergone similar crises and liberation. And after so many momentous discoveries, how disappointed I would be to meet her again, my mind full of 'perversions' and to find her as fantasy-free, self-effacing and compliant as ever. Here was an insoluble dilemma, which I hoped would solve itself somehow when I reached England – though I now felt more pessimistic at the prospect of my return.

But the image of Clarissa gave me a new direction for

my analysis, and I returned to my seat on the lawn and continued to write, under the heading *ARE ALL WOMEN FANTASISTS?* I began with the audacious statement, 'Fantasy is the privilege of the few'.

It appears that most women go through life with their sexual partner(s) without ever having the chance, or finding the courage, to realise their full sexuality through the development and enactment of fantasies. A qualification has to be made here: is it not in the nature of fantasy to be unrealisable? Strictly speaking, the answer must be 'Yes', since fantasy, like dreams, is an imaginary dimension removed from reality. But, using the term more broadly, people can be said to enact versions of their fantasies, even if these usually fall short of the imaginary prototype. So the question is, do women have independent fantasies at all and, secondly, do they ever enact them? We can be sure that the answer to the second question is 'Rarely', because so pervasive is male fantasy and dominance that women have little opportunity to promote their own desires, being indoctrinated with male fantasies which they accept as their own, or are forced to submit to. But the existence of some rare brothels where prostitutes parade their fantasies and clients acquiesce (I hoped this did not break my vow of secrecy) suggests female fantasy is a living force.

The question whether all women have fantasies which they cannot enact is not easy to answer empirically since it deals with the most secretive corners of the mind. Again, the ideological element is deceptive; many women, when asked, admit to sharing macho or violent fantasies, presumably because they have been so thoroughly exposed to them by their partners. Some women, however, confess to fantasies that can certainly be classified as 'non-male' (i.e. which depart from the various archetypes of male sexuality). Those who think that women lack sexual imagination or distinctive fantasies of their own should certainly look to the predominance of male values in our culture for an explanation and not to the supposed barrenness of women's imagination. Before anyone claims that his partner is unimaginative, let him examine his own behaviour and see if he does not ceaselessly force her to participate in his own dream world, drowning her independent imagination.

Unevenly written through this paragraph was, it contained the germ of my conclusions on the subject, and only needed fleshing out to form a respectable hypothesis – or so I hoped.

It was now past midday, and I went to shower and dress for lunch. The formality of the invitation and the use of the woman's surname suggested that it was an occasion for correct dress, and for my striped tie. I went to my assignation looking rather dashing, I thought, and showing no signs of the physical exhaustion which the previous day warranted. I found my way to 'the red room', alias Room 7, and knocked. To my surprise, the door was opened by Virginie, who proceeded to announce me formally to the woman who sat on a chair by the open window. She turned casually and waved me to sit down opposite her. The room was furnished in a style far more stately than any other part of the house, with velvet-upholstered settee and chairs in deep red, a number of antique tables and cabinets, and old framed pictures on the red walls. It seemed anomalous – as if the designer had decided to reproduce a nineteenth-century drawing room in miniature.

The woman who greeted me was not out of keeping with her surroundings, for she looked a typical *haute bourgeoise*, with the elaborate grooming which is typical of that class. Her face was long, almost Grecian, with heavy-lidded eyes and a condescending expression (this seems to be a general hazard for the long-nosed, I notice). Her mouth, however, was wide and sensuous and hinted at a certain *nostalgie de la boue* against which her other features seemed to struggle. Her long, fair hair, expertly streaked with silver, was banished into a pleat at the back of her head. Her dress was cotton, printed with the black-and-white geometrical patterns currently popular, but was unmistakably from one of the best fashion houses – I guessed Chanel – and outlined a trim body with a large bust. She wore stockings with silver seams and high, peep-toe shoes. This woman, like Chloe, seemed ageless, but while Chloe had the agelessness of true beauty, Madame Duchamp had the agelessness of true class. Her face would not appear among the models in *Vogue*, but would undoubtedly be found decorating the gossip column. From the moment I saw her, she reminded me irresistibly of the horse-faced woman in the video-film who was so ill-used at the cocktail party.

I sat facing her and Virginie disappeared to the next room where she started clattering dishes. Madame Duchamp said, 'Do help yourself to a Scotch,' with another casual, scornful wave of her hand, which this time pointed somewhere over my left shoulder. At first I had no clue as to what behaviour was expected of me: should I act the gentleman, as she seemed to be acting the *grande dame*, or the rake? I was dressed rakishly, and this role was most congenial to me, since I am always irked by haughty manners, and secretly long to humble them. And I am too unsure of myself and my sense of self-irony to rely on acting the gentleman. So I launched myself into my part directly by taking half a tumbler of whisky for myself and pouring out about half an inch for her. I also noticed some cigars on the drinks tray and put one ostentatiously into my breast pocket. She accepted her drink with a quizzical glance at mine, then asked for ice. 'There isn't any,' I lied, feeling too idle to go and fetch the ice bucket which stood by the whisky bottle.

'Now, Monsieur Smith, I must have a serious conversation with you. Since I arrived yesterday, I have watched you on all the various video-films, and I have a fair idea of your sexual inclinations.'

'What conclusions do you draw?' I was genuinely intrigued, since I had no inkling how I might appear to others.

'Why, that you are for the most part gentle, pliable, perhaps not typically male in your readiness to acquiesce in women's games, but that somewhere in you lurks a violent streak. When you wore the devil's mask, for example . . . Am I right?'

I congratulated her on an accurate reading, but said that the compliant side of my character was conscious and permanent, while the violent impulses only erupted infrequently, momentarily.

'It is precisely your violent impulses that interest me. But shall we go in to lunch?'

190

She held out her arm for me to take and we passed into the next room, a smaller room painted dark green and containing little more than a large oval dining table. Virginie had set this with a full contingent of china and silver, as if for a five-course meal, and a number of hot and cold dishes stood at the side of the table. When I had seated my companion, whose expectations of gallantry were very high, I served her, then myself, with fish soup and *bordeaux blanc*, again giving myself twice the amount that I allowed her.

'Would I be right,' she asked, 'in thinking that you are ashamed of your outbursts of sexual violence, such as they are?'

'Absolutely,' I replied.

'Yet there *is* a place for violence in sex if the partner is willing, *n'est-ce pas*?'

'I suppose so,' I said. 'But it seems to go along with the sort of macho fantasies that I am trying to escape and that I repudiate. Isn't violence antithetical to the gentle feyness of women's sexual imagination?'

'You underestimate us, Monsieur,' she laughed. 'Let us take the example of rape, which we can probably agree is the archetype of sexual violence. If a man fantasises about rape, he is the central actor in his dream, and the woman is no more than a cunt, an object which he forces to submit. But a woman can fantasise about rape without capitulating to machismo or violence; in *her* fantasy, the man is an object too, the mere instrument by which she is forced to accede to her true, uninhibited sexuality. Because he is the creature of her fantasy, of course, he is not a violent stranger with knife or razor, but an impersonal element of pure chaos which takes her by storm. Do you follow me?'

'I think so,' I said dubiously, wondering where all this was leading.

'What I am saying is that a woman can have an all-female fantasy about rape in a context where she is ultimately in control. The horror of rape in real life is that she has no control over the physical violence which threatens her, hence the moral outrage. The act of penetration is renamed "violation" in consequence.'

I was fascinated by her comments because I had long been vexed as to what I should say about rape in my book. If a woman could fantasise about rape with herself as subject rather than object, perhaps she was not just the dupe of male delusions of power and strength.

'To speak more bluntly still, Monsieur Smith, this fantasy of rape in a controlled situation is one of my own, and this is why I've asked you to lunch.'

It took me some time to digest this information. So, I had been invited here as a potential rapist. Up till now, I had felt no pressing desire to do anything sexual to Madame Duchamp, not because she was not sexy – she was – but because her frigid and haughty demeanour had repelled me and diverted me to a non-sexual repertoire of polite behaviour. When I realised that I could treat her as a mere victim or object, so that I would have no need to *relate* to this alien creature (as psychologists say), I felt considerably more enthusiastic – besides which, the wine was making me feel randy. All the same, the order, 'Rape me', is almost as self-defeating as the demand, 'Surprise me'. I wondered what incident could trigger off my sadistic impulses. We continued eating and I finished the bottle of white wine and helped myself generously to some claret, recalling that alcohol and crimes of violence are statistically linked. Madame

Duchamp went on to talk of neutral subjects, asking me what exhibitions I had seen in Paris, and what theatres I had visited. After her brief revelation, she had reverted to her grand manner.

When lunch was over, by which time I felt pleasantly drunk, we took cups of coffee back to the other room and sat down together on the sofa. I found myself slipping into a parody of the seducer, and complimenting her extravagantly on her appearance and dress. Her answers were modest, non-commital, but her teasing tone of voice led me on. I took her hand and played with it for a long time, noticing the expensive platinum rings which studded each finger, and then I rested my hand lightly on her knee, insinuating my fingers a few inches under her skirt, over a firm thigh. Her stockings were silk, pleasing to the touch. So far she did not protest at all at this familiarity.

Continuing with my quaintly old-fashioned, Don-Juanesque approach, I leant over and kissed her and, while I did so, removed my hand from her knee and held her breast tightly. I could feel its moulded, constricted volume – she was wearing a bra. So much the better. She pushed my trespassing hand away, but as I kissed her mouth harder it wilfully returned, and started to unbutton the front of her dress. Her verbal protests I muffled with my probing tongue, and her hand, which tried to drag mine away, was too weak for my determined strength. However, as I pushed through the gap I had made and dug my fingers with professional skill into the top of her bra-cup, feeling a wealth of soft, shivering flesh there, she slapped my face very hard. That was the trigger, for I cannot experience physical pain without an immediate urge to retaliate. To be slapped by such an

193

affected, long-nosed bitch! I hit her back hard, a rakish response which she did not expect, then leapt at her like an animal, and tore down the top half of her dress, revealing her to be exceptionally well-stacked (size 38,C cup, I mentally noted). She was too surprised by my sudden attack to take evasive, or mock-evasive, action and I seized her by the wrists and, tugging off my neck-tie, tied her hands behind her back. I made her lie lengthwise on the sofa, and loomed above her, menacing her.

'Don't make any noise, or I'll break your neck,' I warned. What had begun as play-acting had turned into a real desire to violate and degrade this woman, showing my contempt for her and the way of life which she represented.

I calculated where to begin my assault. I left her dress dangling from her waist because it looked so ridiculous – also, because it left me the chance of a brutal, below-belt attack later. Taking out my nail-scissors from my inside pocket, I took hold of the bra and, pulling its fabric away from her tit, I cut a small hole in the centre, through which I roughly pulled her nipple – and then did the same to her left-hand breast. An isolated nipple is an innately absurd object, and I poked them both casually, this way and that, then fell to pinching them very hard, which had her rolling her eyes in anguish. Nevertheless, the brown buttons grew hard with my offensive. Then I lay on top of her, carelessly digging my knee into her stomach, and bit each nipple viciously hard, until she sobbed (very softly), making some appeal for clemency. My scissors came out again, and this time I cut both the bra straps and the thin elastic strip joining the two cups together, and peeled off her protective covering like an

194

eggshell. Her large breasts spread outwards luxuriantly, and the sight of the exposed mounds of flesh drove me wild with the impulse to crush and hurt. I pressed down on them with all my might, trying to flatten and erase them, while areas of errant flesh irrepressibly poked through my spread fingers or bulged out beyond my hands' reach. Then I pulled them into strange shapes, lifting and dropping them abruptly, while I said aloud to her, scathingly, that Marilyn Monroe could get away with that sort of thing, but that breasts like balloons looked absurd on someone of her age. She whimpered, but her body seemed to move in rhythm as I manipulated the magnificent mountains.

Below her waist was an unseen territory, ready for devastation. I resisted the temptation to cut open the skirt of her expensive dress, out of some lingering respect for what money could buy, and undid the zip which kept it tight at the waist, pulling it up to her neck so that it covered her eyes. Now I saw only her body as an object for my sadistic fancies, and not her pleading, human face. She wore a suspender belt over black lace panties, and I took a vandal's pleasure in cutting the belt to pieces. It left its elastic imprints over the pale globe of her well-filled stomach, and I paused to give that vulnerable expanse a violent massage, omitting the preliminary caresses and concentrating on the pounding of the final stage. Now I pulled down her stockings and took off her shoes. My victim was mute. I ran the points of my open scissors from her toes, over the soles of her feet and up her inside leg and thigh – a ticklish process, it seemed from her gasps.

Then I turned her on her side, bending up her legs. With a tailor's accuracy, I snipped a hole in her pants some two inches round to allow me access to her cunt, and another which vacated the way to her arse. And then, with no warning at all, I jabbed two fingers into the first hole, and my thumb into the second, and screwed and frigged them around. She moaned and shook her shoulders, trying perhaps to shake off the dress which smothered her and obscured her visual anticipation of what inroads I might make next. For a time I enjoyed the brutal, mechanical play of my hands inside her: my fingers were now wet with her dew and slipped easily in and out, but my thumb ground round relentlessly in the dry, arid hole of her arse, try as it might to expel the intruder.

The purity of this experience of woman-as-object was remarkable: I was not troubled by the sight of those parts of her body, like the clitoris, which selfishly demand attention, but was directed with the undistracted accuracy of a flying arrow into the orifices where I myself would find gratification.

'Now, you pompous cow,' I growled, 'You haven't seen the half of it. I'm going to fuck you till you split in two!'

She wailed piteously. I put her on her back again, and lifted her right leg over the sofa's back, and let the left one dangle over its edge. Then, kneeling between their wide gap, I prepared for the rape, touching my cock the way it excites me most. Such preparation was hardly needed, since from the beginning of my seductive tactics I had been vaguely conscious of having a hard-on, although my attention had been focussed on my victim's pangs rather than my own sensations. My rigid cock slid through the hole in her pants, enjoying the sense of double penetration. Now I modelled myself on the

196

pneumatic drill and pierced her cunt with such sharp, vibrant strokes that my heart was soon pounding like the generator of that obscene energy which I was expending in her degradation. I sensed, rather than heard, her suppressed cries at the violent incursion. When I had spent myself temporarily, I came out of her and considered what to do next.

My natural inventiveness came to my aid. I remembered seeing some suitable instrument on the lunch table and went off to find it, my trousers flapping round my knees. On the table was a monstrous silver pepper-pot, smooth and shiny, shaped like a fat rocket, standing on ornate, claw-like legs. It was as large as my cock, and certainly more erect after its own fashion. I went back silently and found her just as I had left her, legs wide apart, begging for – what? Without warning, I plunged the pepper-pot through the hole in her pants, into her cunt. It was a tight squeeze at first, but its pointed rocket's nose soon forced a trajectory up her passage and the rest of it followed. Cautious no longer of my threats of violence, she screamed at the shock of the cold metal. But her scream seemed tinged with something other than pain. Soon, she was wet, and the thing fitted so snugly that it crossed my mind that its appearance on the lunch-table had not just been coincidence.

I manoeuvred the impromptu dildo in and out, twisting it around and changing the pace unpredictably, which made her shudder. I wondered idly if pepper would have the same catastrophic effect on the soft membranes of the vagina as it does on the sister-membranes of the nose. I looked forward to witnessing a vaginal sneeze, but it never came. The pot was empty, I realised – and not by accident, surely. I was conscious that my victim was getting increasingly excited as the pepper-pot moved to a speedy crescendo inside her. The rapist, I discovered, becomes instantly more sadistic if he suspects his victim of enjoyment. So I stopped my activities in that area, leaving the pepper-pot right inside her cunt, with only the claw-legs poking out between her labia, and turned her over, so that for the first time both of her plump, moonlike buttocks were visible together, gazing dumbly up at me. I beat a sharp tatoo on them with the hard heels of my hands, then set about the ultimate act of rape. Although my purpose had formerly been to abuse her in every way imaginable, by now I was eager to gratify myself too, to come in her and over her, and smother her with my spunk.

My cock was at its biggest, and hard as wood, and her arse-hole was singularly tight and unyielding, partly because the pepper-pot which filled and expanded her other passage had greatly contracted this one. But determination paid dividends and, with only a few Herculean thrusts, I was able to enter her and wallow in that tropical cavern whose dirty walls pressed ever closer around me, thanks to the nearby dildo. As soon as I began to bugger her in earnest the friction on my aching cock was so intense that it turned my movements into very slow motion. I could hear groans of pain or pleasure from under the dress but paid no attention, for now my only focus of sensation was the fierce pressure which compressed and elongated my cock as it moved in the narrow passage. After a few raids on this sacred spot, I was stirred by raging lust, and found myself at the moment of climax, or even beyond. As I thrust myself in again and she cried out once more, her arse clamped me in a painful spasm and squeezed out every drop of spunk in great contractions.

I was smitten by post-coital spite, not sadness, and was tempted to leave her just as she was, with her hands still tied up, so that she would be found in that ludicrous and humiliating state by the maid – how are the mighty fallen! But I wanted my tie back, so I released her hands, rescued the pepper-pot, which had nearly vanished into her cunt, and left her to put the rest to rights. At first, she did not speak or move under the dress, although I could hear her rasping breath. Had she enjoyed my fierce usage – had she come, as those last strangled cries suggested? I did not particularly care. She had certainly got what she asked for, I told myself. I pulled up my trousers, stepped over the detritus of ruined underwear beside the sofa and went towards the door. The body on the sofa stirred languorously and her husky, classy voice called after me mockingly 'Not bad at all. With a little practice, Monsieur Smith, you might make quite a good rapist! *Adieu!*' I left the red room, trying to affect the jaunty air of one who has had his way.

When I arrived back it was about four o'clock and I lay down on the bed. I was surprised to discover that I was shaking from some inner coldness created by the savage interlude. When I thought about it, I was ashamed to remember my readiness to become the violator when given carte blanche, and to take class revenge on a passive woman's body. Perhaps one of my own fantasies which I had hitherto concealed from myself was really that of degradation and rape. Yet what had ensued was not in any legal sense a rape, since my victim had indicated her consent – indeed, she had literally asked for it, and forced the aggressor's role on me so that, in the sense that she had described, she was ultimately in control of the situation. She alone had been the author of the fantasy even if I had added a few details of my own. The subjugation and violation that she had undergone was, I concluded, a far cry from being pulled by an unknown hand wielding a knife into a dark alley or onto a vacant lot, and fucked against one's will. In retrospect, and without too much hypocrisy, I decided to exonerate myself. I also knew that she had given me an invaluable analysis of how women fantasise about rape without capitulating to the male fantasy of the same name, *and* without offering any justification to the criminal rapist. My pleasure in the situation had, I reflected, been heightened immensely by the knowledge that I was desecrating that formal bourgeois drawing-room, as well as her aristocratic arse and cunt, and exposing the falsehood of her affected manners. Something about upper-class confidence cries out to be violated – why doesn't it happen more often?

Feeling calmer and warmer after this heart-searching, I went into my sitting-room for one last enjoyable session with the titillating television circuit. As I glanced out of my window I was surprised to see that the expensive green car had already disappeared. The whore vanishes – and fast. The TV circuit seemed to have a secret empathy with my own wishes, for when I switched on it immediately transported me back to the exotic room where I had enjoyed a thousand and one delights the night before. The shrouded white figure was busy massaging my body and I appraised my figure stretched out on the couch with considerable satisfaction. Only when you see yourself thus reified in a film or photograph can you appreciate how you appear to others. There seemed to be two or three cameras in simultaneous operation in the room, concealed behind the tapestries, no doubt, because shots at different angles were intercut. Lalande's sudden appearance impressed me even more than it had at the time, for now I was able to regard his magnificent physique with its stark, uncompromising blackness objectively, and feel its true sensual power. The culmination of the film was, of course, our joint enjoyment of the enslaved prostitute, a slow entanglement of fair and dark limbs which had a singular dynamic beauty. When you are participating in a sexual act, you miss the extraordinary visual dimension which elevates the mere animal act to an aesthetic plane, more properly called lovemaking. Even strategic mirrors cannot afford the enjoyment of each angle and the ever-changing configuration of flesh and bone which so intrigue the voyeur. A camera in the ceiling looked down on Lalande and I entwined with the girl and each other in a slow, perpetual motion, like an animated Hindu god with multiple limbs, until the shuddering climax and the gradual separation of this deity of lust into his three components parts.

I would have switched off again, fully content with the bodily poetry which I had just witnessed, but the title of the next film captured my attention, *Love Among the Snakes*. The film was again old and jerky, perhaps dating from the early twenties since Wiene's *Caligari* seemed to have influenced the sets with their sinister painted shadows and distorted perspectives. The context was a fairground, a riot of movement and activity, and the camera followed a young man, dashingly dressed in striped suit and cravat, who meandered round looking curiously at the sideshows. Finally, he came to a stall entitled 'The Snake Woman' and paid his money to go inside. We followed him up wooden stairs through heavy, dark curtains and onto a raised platform which formed three sides of a square round a sunken tank with a glass lid. Inside, a naked girl was reclining on a long cushion with fair hair which swept down to her thighs and hung over her naked body, concealing everything except the swelling of her breasts. The camera showed her from some height above; the moment of true horror was when it swooped down into close-up and showed that her hair was that of a Gorgon. In and out of the long tresses slithered innumerable snakes, some long and thin, some short and swollen, absurdly phallic. Several snakes were wound about her wrists and arms, and a large boa constrictor was wrapped around her thigh in multiple coils, his tail poking up between her legs. The constant serpentine activity did not in the least disturb the girl, who was calmly reading an illustrated paper, occasionally displacing a few of her reptilian playmates as she turned the page.

The young man was thunderstruck by the sight; he leaned over the barrier and peered at her as closely as he could. He walked round and round to inspect her from all angles, and tried to catch her attention by knocking on the lid of her vivarium, but she steadfastly refused to look up. Other curiosity-seekers came through and pushed past him, but he did not notice. Finally, he fell to staring at her with an expression of total infatuation until the showman appeared through the curtains and gesticulated to him to get out as the show, apparently, was closing for the day. He left reluctantly, his eyes turned backwards and downwards. The camera briefly followed his dejected walk home and his solitary supper in the kitchen of an elegant apartment, then it cut back to the deserted fairground late at night. The beam of a torch picked out the garishly ornamented sign 'The Snake Woman'. Sure enough, it was held by the young man. Although the doors to the show had been secured, he had brought some kind of implement which soon forced them open, and he was inside. His spotlight wandered round the room and discovered a switch, which he put on, flooding the room with light.

The girl was asleep in her tank, lying on her side, still covered with a sheet of blonde hair, but the light startled her awake and she looked up in terror. The torpid snakes were also aroused, and soon they were winding and unwinding, seething over her body in rage at this disturbance. Meanwhile the interloper threw off his clothes and climbed the barrier, lifting the glass lid, and stepped daringly in beside her. The camera moved down again and focussed on the two. The girl seemed by no means displeased at this intrusion and sat up, holding out her arms to him, and he joined her in a fierce embrace, while the snakes swarmed over this new, alien body, and seemed to cover every inch of him with their living mass. Although I was on tenterhooks, as the film-maker no doubt intended, waiting for them to deliver the death-bite, I soon realised that their fangs must have been drawn, as is the custom in such shows. The snakes did not deter the lover from kissing his Gorgon ardently. As her hair fell from her body and she lay back to enjoy his caresses, her graceful shape was revealed, with prominent breasts, round one of which a snake lay coiled neatly, as if in a basket. The lover turned aside for a moment, trying to disentangle his cock from a small, lithe snake which had mistaken its rigidity for that of a friendly stick, and was coiled round it. Eventually he freed himself and lay down covering the girl and began to make love to her, while snakes slipped coolly in between their entwined bodies. This Garden of Eden idyll went on rather too long. The director was, I thought, relying heavily on the intrinsic vileness of his subject. And vile it was, to see hundreds of snaky parodies of the human penis insinuating themselves into the many gaps between the heaving bodies.

The climax was unexpected, inhuman. All this time, the great boa constrictor had been sleeping piled up in a corner, but now he raised his fearsome head, his forked tongue flickering in and out – perhaps he was jealous. He uncoiled and slithered across the tank, revealing his great length, some eight feet or more, and passed under the arched waist of the girl, then round that of the man, then under the girl again. The camera could not indicate the immense pressure with which he joined the lovers in their death embrace – it only showed their movements subsiding, their arms and legs writhing wildly, snakelike, and then being flung out in their final agony. Then there was stillness. But the snakes danced on over the dead lovers.

The Philosopher in the Last Boudoir

The reputed hynoptic powers of the snake must be transmissible even on celluloid, for I was powerfully affected by this scene and remained sunk in my chair for long afterwards, imagining dry, scaly forms creeping over my flesh. The film had been a long one, and the evening sun now shone through my window. It would soon be dinner time. I bathed and dressed myself, sad to think that this was the last time I would go through this careful ritual. When I entered the dining-room, Madame greeted me warmly. She wore the black dress which suited her so well, and was looking radiantly young. Perhaps Lalande's care for her health went beyond that of a physician. We sat down at once to eat the plate of *charcuterie* which was already on the table.

'I gather that you are leaving tomorrow, Monsieur Smith.' (So even my phone calls were overheard.) Madame went on, 'I shall be upset to see you go, I have enjoyed our dinners together so much. I love the conversation of intelligent men, especially Englishmen. And you, has your time here been profitable?'

'Beyond measure,' I answered. 'With the information I have gathered here I'm sure I can finish my book in another month or so. And the things that you have told me have been invaluable. I shall always be grateful.'

These formalities over, we served ourselves with the *provençal* stew from a black iron pot on the table.

'You have often asked me about the women here, Monsieur Smith, and so far I have avoided answering your inquiries. But I think that before you leave I shall share with you the secrets of my house. I can see that you are a discreet man and a foreigner – so that no harm will come from the revelation.

'Please tell me,' I said, delighted at the idea of uncovering the mystery which had so long intrigued me.

'The women whom you have met are not really prostitutes.'

'*Not* prostitutes. Then who are they?'

'They are Parisiennes who are bored with the monotony of monogamy, or with a conventional sex life where they are dominated by men's lusts and chauvinistic male fantasies. They seek to escape phallocracy, as we call it. They come here for refreshment, to enjoy the realisation of their dreams and the liberation of their true sexuality. You might call them feminists, though most of them are not so in the formal sense of the word. Perhaps they enjoy sex too much to accede to the self-denial which feminists so often prescribe as a defence against men. Their way is to control men, not to avoid them altogether.'

I was astounded, and yet not entirely surprised, for none of the women had seemed like tarts, even when

206

they behaved most like whores. How strange – my original supposition had been right, that women's fantasies are whores' fantasies, and vice versa.

'What sort of women are they, then?'

'Women of good class, you could say, for I won't accept any others, and some of them are my personal friends. Among the women you met, for example, is a wealthy young heiress. She is so sick of the sexual overtures made to her by exploitative men who want to reach her money through her body, that she comes here to remind herself that sex can be free and fulfilling, untainted by social and commercial manoeuvrings. She goes back determined to resist her suitors and to fulfil herself sexually. Perhaps she will never marry, thanks to me, but will live the life of a free woman.' I tried to identify her – Julie, the garden girl? There were several possibilities. 'Who else?'

'Naturally, I can't reveal their names. But you have seen a model of international fame, and a distinguished university professor – and a titled lady married to a pig of a nobleman whose only thought is to get drunk and masturbate over her, before falling into a stupor. Many of these women, in another setting, would be instantly recognisable as *haute bourgeoisie*, but here they leave that sort of label behind them.'

Chloe was the model, of course – I knew I had seen her face. As to the others, the descriptions were too vague for me to be able to place them. The fantasy of women is exceptionally free because of its separation from social roles and status, whereas men cannot forget their pompous lives even in the secret refuge of the bedroom. But this made identification impossible.

'The other thing which I know has intrigued you is the

existence of the nearby village, and its absentee inhabitants. Most of the women who come here to amuse themselves have bought or built houses in the village so that they can come as often as they need to, without exciting the suspicions of their husbands and lovers. The ruse succeeds admirably, and in addition they have made a nice investment in property which will one day be worth a lot.'

'When your house becomes a museum of sexual liberation and feminist tourists flock here from all over the world?'

'Perhaps,' she smiled. 'And, since I have decided to tell you everything, I should add that these women pay *me* handsomely for the facilities which I provide. I shall not finish my old age in poverty.'

I laughed loud and long, to think that the sum I had paid Madame de Rochevillier would have been multiplied many times by the time I left, thanks to my own efforts. I felt the piquant admiration which is inspired by the revelation of any large-scale con-trick. This astute double-agent of prostitution impressed me even more than before.

We had finished our meal and sat back in armchairs with brandy and coffee as so often before. I felt replete with food, and with the pleasures of the week, but the sensation of having been exploited, although I bore no resentment, made me review our transaction with a new, calculating eye.

'I seem to remember, Madame, that when I arrived you promised me ten girls in ten rooms. To the best of my knowledge, I have only had nine, so far.'

'You are quite right,' she replied. 'Now you have seen all the rooms but mine. Let us go to my room.'

A strange thrill ran through me. With the overweening hubris of the young, I had in theory no desire to fuck a seventy-year-old woman, however beautiful and well-preserved. Yet in practice, I found Madame's physical presence nagged and tantalised me despite, or perhaps because of, the prohibition of age which so cruelly classifies us into the sexual and the non-sexual. So I was on my feet at once, abandoning my glass of brandy, and followed her up the main stairs to a door in the centre of the house which I had never entered before. This was Madame's bedroom. The room was enormous, with a thickly piled white carpet which seemed to stretch to infinity. At the far end was a great white bed. There were one or two plain pinewood chairs and a hi-fi with some records standing on a low table. Nothing else. Madame closed the door and turned to me.

'Shall I tell you one more fantasy? The ultimate fantasy of a woman is still to love and be loved when she is old.' I understood and I nodded agreement, but there was something I had to ask, even though I feared to embarrass her.

'Do you and Lalande . . .?'

'Of course. He is the young man of whom I spoke, older now. Although he may have seemed unsympathetic to you, almost too buoyantly masculine, he has a childlike desire to please women and to satisfy them.'

I sat down on a chair, still unsure of my duties here, and she went to the stereo and put on a record. The wistful notes of a Debussy sonata for piano and violin filled the room, and she started to undo her dress, talking as she did so.

'In my youth I was a ballerina – not perhaps a great

one, but much admired. I went under the name of Katya Asnarova. Had I not married I might have become a star of world renown, but my first husband feared I would be seduced by the bohemian life of the stage, and stolen from him. So he stopped me dancing. Since then I have only danced for my friends. Now I shall dance for you.'

Her dress fell to the floor and she stood erect, with dignity in her nakedness. I saw with surprise that she wore no underclothes. Her figure had always seemed so trim that I thought she must be tightly corsetted, but I could now see that her muscles were still taut, and guarded the slim shape of her tall body, despite advancing age. From a distance it was the body of a woman of forty or so, without the elasticity of youth, but still a lovely shape. Only when I was closer did I see the small wrinkles and puckers left by the passage of time. She put her hands to her head and took out some invisible pins, and the hair which I had only seen drawn back in a chignon fell to her shoulders thick and white. She was a strange, haunting sight, but the large blue eyes which seemed to hold her soul fixed mine intensely, as if challenging me to feel amusement or pity.

Then she began to dance: her steps were informal, attuned to the indeterminate ramblings of the romantic music. I saw her strong, ballerina's legs lift high in the air. Although she no longer performed the leaps and pirouettes of her youth, the dance ritual which I saw was infinitely graceful and rivetting for the spectator. The hair under her arms was still dark, I saw when she raised them, so was the thick cluster between her legs. I was transfixed by her dance; she too seemed mesmerised by her own movement and her eyes were far away. As I watched I mechanically began to take off my clothes so

210

that by the end of the record I stood naked by the chair, still entranced, and scarcely thinking of my own body, so absorbed had I been in the lovely acrobatics which her limbs performed. I had felt it disrespectful to be clothed while she was naked, and some part of me wanted to feel my skin against hers, to achieve that final intimacy which only belongs to two naked bodies, even if I never made love to her.

She turned off the music and I went over and took her in my arms in a long embrace, kissing her shoulders and breasts, which were still round and liquid, not the reputedly parched breasts of old age. Her hands felt me all over, tremulously, and I realised that, hardened though she might be by her commerce in sex, she had been fearful of my reaction, afraid that I would repulse her after such heart-rending self-exposure. I caressed her with redoubled tenderness and felt my cock harden and yearn towards her. Perhaps she did not want sex, only affection – yet I wanted a consummation of our new closeness. I led her over to the bed and she made no protest but lay down at my side, while I ran my hands here and there on her body, and finally dared to reach between her legs and let my hand linger on her cunt. It made its way between the lips. She was moist there, not unwilling to receive me, and be taken. As if in a dream, I lay on top of her and penetrated her secrets, finding a honeyed welcome in a cunt whose elasticity was undiminished, and which held me close. With my arms round her, and kissing her full mouth, I fucked her slowly, then fast, and felt her body vibrate with excitement and grow warm in my embrace until, after what seemed like hours of blissful motion, she came with one loud cry. My own pleasure had been so attached to hers, growing out of it like the sucker from the rose, until it reached its own maturity, that when her orgasm was over I came at once with a wet sweetness that obliterated everything else. We lay still for a long time, while I kissed every inch of her face and looked into her blue eyes, searching for forgiveness if I had violated her mysteries too thoroughly. When her eyes finally focussed on mine she smiled and said, 'Now you see how easy it is to gratify an old woman's fantasy.'

'The pleasure was all mine,' I said, with sincere humility.

'I won't forget you. But I am tired now, so I must ask you to go. I doubt if I shall see you before you leave. A good journey to England, and good luck with your book. If you can tell the world the secrets of female sexuality, you will have performed a great service to one half of humanity. Goodbye, Monsieur Smith.'

I kissed her mouth again, and then her hand, and left her lying naked on the white coverlet, her flowing white hair fanned out on the pillow, her great wise eyes closed in tranquillity, age joined with innocence. I felt more drained emotionally than physically, but when I got back to my room I too fell into bed in a state of total exhaustion.

Parting Meetings

When Virginie brought in my breakfast at the unusually early hour of seven, I told her that I was leaving, and a shadow seemed to cross her face. Of relief, perhaps, since I had hardly been a satisfying companion. I asked her to ring for a taxi to pick me up at nine-thirty, so I could catch the train at ten. The weather had changed and was heavy and grey: town weather, I thought, and suddenly longed to be away from this bleak countryside. I washed and dressed thoughtfully, unable to forget the unexpected episode with Madame de Rochevillier which now, in retrospect, seemed like the logical culmination of all the strange experiences of the week. If a man can accept the fantasy and the sexuality of an old woman – as women are forced to do in the case of 'dirty old men' – surely he is no longer a chauvinist. What it means is that he accepts that a woman may lust after him when he has no reciprocal desires – a fact which most men find it convenient to ignore, although they will happily press on with their attentions when the asymmetry operates in reverse.

I packed my bags quickly and then wondered how to occupy the intervening hour or so before my departure. I took out my notebook again and sat at the table to make a few notes on this new insight, but after a moment I was interrupted by Virginie who arrived with dustpan and brush, and announced that she had to clean the room for the next arrival. I thought this was too precipitate. 'Can't you wait until I've gone? I'll only be here another hour,' I said, in some irritation.

'Sorry, Monsieur, Madame's orders,' she said, as if that closed the question. I resigned myself to having her bustling around me and concentrated on my notes. But soon my attention was caught by the unconventional fashion in which Virginie set about her task. Although such a house must have boasted several vacuum cleaners, she bent double, teetering on her stiletto heels, and brushed the dirt from the carpet into the pan. It was an extraordinary performance, and seemed very inefficient, since no dirt reached her pan. When I first noticed her doing this, some atavistic, prudish instinct made me look away instantly, for the mini-skirt which composed her uniform today was raised right over her rump. Then I look back again rapidly, because despite my subliminally swift glance, information filtered through to my brain to the effect that something was wrong. As she moved on and bent down again, her back to me, I saw that she wore no knickers, and that two gloriously round, peach-coloured buttocks were pointed straight at me. She was bent into such a hairpin shape that between them I could see a fair fuzz of hair and the pink lips of her cunt. Black suspenders ran down the tops of her thighs and fastened her stockings. Since Virginie's arse had always attracted my notice, I stared openmouthed as she straightened up, moved on and bent down again, moving round me in a wide semi-circle as she swept, always keeping her arse pointing straight at me, the notional centre of her circle. My eyes travelled with her round its diameter.

Soundlessly, I undid my flies and found my cock hard with mischievous anticipation. Silently, I stood up and crept up behind her, brandishing my cock at her, and pointing at its pink target. And suddenly, I grasped her hips in both my hands and rushed into her, as if drawn by a magnet deep inside. She gasped with surprise, then gave her provocative laugh and said, 'At last!' I kept her bending there for a long time, while my cock bounded joyously in and out of her wide-open, deep, liquid cunt, and I slapped her engaging buttocks with my palms. What had begun as a 'What the Butler Saw' episode soon became an erotic adventure. I reached over her with my arms and tore off the lace cap she habitually wore, and saw her fair hair cascade down to reach the floor. Then, reaching under her, I felt for the buttons of her blouse and undid them. Her long breasts hung forward at a strange angle and I palpated them greedily. The heavy smell of musk and sweat which surrounded her swept over me, exciting yet another of my five senses. Meanwhile, I was intoxicated by my own slithering in and out of the silky envelope of her cunt, and felt myself about to come. But I wanted to delay the moment and to feed on her pornographic body, which was so much less ragged and used than I had painted it in my imagination. In fact, as I hastily tore off the rest of her clothes, I realised that she could not be more than twenty-one.

Thick cosmetics and old-fashioned clothes had deluded me into thinking she was an aging whore, but with her fair hair flung over her breasts and her eyes wide open with excitement, she seemed to me the epitome of youth and temptation. I was hungry for the eating of this magic fruit which had so tantalisingly sprung out of my reach for a whole week.

While undressing her I left on her white apron — fetishism, but who cares? Dressed only in that she was a wonderful amalgam of decorousness and naughtiness. In a few seconds, my own clothes were off and I pulled her into the bedroom and threw her on the bed, being rougher than I intended in my amorous haste, but she seemed pleased, and clung to me tightly. I buried my head under her apron, licking the white, soft curve of her belly, then chewing my way downwards into her cunt. Her hands were at my neck, and ruffled and pulled my hair. My tongue ran up and down the lips of her cunt, and drank the strong, salty liquor which was already oozing between them, then serpented through them and played on her clitoris like the strings of a harp while her voice made musical sounds of delight. By now I was drugged with her smell and her flesh, and drunk with the desire to possess her. I was on top of her again, sucking at her nipples while my hands squeezed her delectable buttocks and my throbbing cock, now crazily aroused, dug once more into her sweet, earthy garden to plant its seed there. Its deepening, spadelike motions made her thrill and shudder in time to my rhythm and she was soon panting, her eyes opening wider at the shock of each thrust. Her long nails clawed my back and drove me wild; my kisses on her breasts turned to savage bites, and so with nails and teeth we goaded each other to a greater frenzy. I gave myself up to an exquisite self-abandonment which made me feel she was turning me inside out and raping me from head to toe. When I was so beside myself with lust that I could delay no longer, I said to her, 'Come, you slut, come now!' and I felt a massive, tumultuous shaking beneath me which took hold of my cock and crushed it so tightly that I came, totally out of control of my spasm, in a violent, wet explosion that splashed over her thighs and filled her cunt full, while it emptied my mind of all but ecstasy. Delayed gratification, says Freud, condemning the pleasure principle, is far sweeter than immediate satisfaction. I had to admit he was right in this case.

But already Virginie had got up from the bed and pointed silently to the clock which said nine thirty-five. 'Georges will wait for you,' she said, 'but you must hurry if you want to catch the train.' As she spoke I heard a car starting up outside the house, and rushed to the window to see it disappearing down the drive. 'Don't worry,' said the omniscient Virginie, 'that's not your car. Georges is waiting at the gate.' She helped me to put on my clothes, not without a little caressing of my empty cock, which her hands had never felt during our breakneck love-making. She had already put on her own clothes and looked demure as ever, save for her tumbling hair which there was no time to put up.

'I will see you to the gate,' she said, and resumed her maid's role, even insisting on carrying my case. As we hastened away, I made a rapid, silent salutation to the house of pleasure. Then I asked Virginie whether she lived and worked here permanently.

'No, only during my vacations,' she said, surprising

me again when I thought I was incapable of further surprise.

'Who acts as maid when you are back at your studies, then?' I asked.

'I have several sisters . . .' she answered enigmatically. I wondered if they were anything like her.

We reached the iron gates which stood open after the departure of the other car, and the taxi was waiting outside, its engine idling. Georges was still smoking his cigar and reading the sports page of *Figaro*. He gave me a nod of recognition. I turned to Virginie and kissed her lightly on both cheeks saying, 'If you ever want to learn English one vacation instead of coming here, Madame can give you my address.' She gave me her wide, temptress's smile, then began to close the gates as I got into the taxi. They clanged shut as we drove off, and the house took on the barred and bolted aspect of an unwilling cunt. Georges drove at high speed to catch the train and did not bother me with any questions about my stay except to ask if I had enjoyed my 'holiday'. I sat back and watched the deserted houses flash past, and wondered where in Paris I might discover their owners, whose faces, cunts and arses I knew so well, but who might seem unrecognisable if I met them in the context of respectability.

We narrowly missed a wandering sheep and almost hit a bus, but at last we careered into the station yard at half a minute to ten. I thrust a hundred franc note at Georges, jumped out of the taxi and rushed over to the waiting train. I got into a small compartment and closed the door just as it pulled out of the station. I lay back on the seat and closed my eyes, my mind a blur of gratified desire and remembered excitements. Only half-an-hour ago, Virginie and I had been rutting away in a haze of musk. And now all those mountains and caves and billows of succulent female flesh were ten kilometres from here, and retreating rapidly as the train gathered speed. But perhaps I could recapture them in my *magnum opus* – or would I instead forgo academic esteem and try to relive those days of debauchery more graphically, in the bluest of blue novels?

A woman's voice disturbed my thoughts with an English, 'Hallo!' I opened my eyes, startled, and looked up. The only other passenger in the compartment was sitting opposite me, a woman with black satin trousers tucked into high boots, with a tight black leather jacket. Her face was hidden behind a large book which I noticed was written in English, entitled *Freud on Fantasy*. The book was lowered, very slowly, and I saw a feline face, almost the face of Chantal, with round luminous eyes. The girl's hair, streaked like a tabby's fur, snaked round high, rouged cheekbones and, on meeting my eyes, she smiled. I saw a mouth full of sharp, tiny teeth – another cat-beauty, but somehow this one reminded me of a tigress.

I asked 'How did you know I was English?'

'By the cut of your suit, of course,' she laughed. 'I live just near Jermyn Street, and I know the signs!' She leaned back, stretching her long legs wide apart, put her book aside, and looked at me – voraciously, I thought. 'Are you going to Paris, then flying to London?'

I said I was.

'So am I.' Her eyes flashed at me with sudden jungle wickedness. 'Do you know, I have always dreamed of being alone in a compartment with a handsome man, with blinds you can draw down –' she pulled one down to

219

show me '– and lights you can put out, like this . . .'

I smelt the danger – I longed to be eaten – I foresaw that I would miss the afternoon plane, and maybe many more.